EARTH

TO

EARTH

A Beginner's Guide To Unwitching

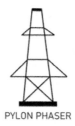

PYLON PHASER

Richard Daniels

A Pylon Phaser publication

Low Scaraby
Lincolnshire
United Kingdom

theoccultaria@gmail.com

www.occultariaofalbion.com

ISBN-13: 978-1-7391508-0-8

Cover design: Melody Phelan-Clark

Contents

The Occultaria Of Albion

A note on the Occultaria of Albion

The OA is a part-work series that explores different locations where hauntings, time-slips, cryptids, curses and all manner of supernatural events have occurred.

It is a mystical collection of the mysterious, a broadcast from a forgotten frequency, another Albion.

In its various editions you will learn about such things as:
- *Unwitchers*
- *The Lost Glove Society*
- *The Nihlex Corporation*
- *The Sinister Sisters Biker Gang*
- *And much more...*

The Occultaria of Albion also exists as a podcast. Each episode investigates and explores more of the OA archives. The podcast is available on most platforms including iTunes and Spotify.

occultariaofalbion.com

'an Unwitcher is a shadow on a summer's day, who is't with stealth, protects this world from those darker realms where only cankered energies dwelleth.'

Omnia Daemonia, 1603

Part 1:

How To Banish A Demon

The wind whirled. In the darkness, as it struck and danced against the immeasurable edges and angles of the cliff face, it sang in a duet with the white noise of the North Sea waves.

Up on the clifftop, set back from its brambled edge, on a bench, a woman sat alone in the orange glow of a nearby lamppost. She listened to the night, her grey, bobbed hair just visible above the collar of an old wax jacket that smelt of earth and bonfires and layers of long-dried Molinard Habanita, her favourite perfume.

A man appeared on the footpath and stepped into the cone of light, quickly sitting down beside the woman. He gave a theatrical toss of his scarf then tucked his hands into the duffle coat he wore with an equally theatrical shiver, though he wasn't feeling cold.

"So, you decided to come," the woman said, not looking at him.

"What choice did I have?"

"You knew there would be consequences to your actions." She sighed and turned her head to him. "You acted like a bloody fool – so don't be sour with me."

"I'm not sour. I'm on some desolate clifftop in Norfolk." He checked his watch. "And it's long after midnight."

Her gaze returned to the cliff edge. "It had to be somewhere out of the way. Besides…"

"You felt like a trip to the seaside? It's probably a bit late for doughnuts."

"Even I can get sick of being in a stuffy office, Jack." She crossed her legs and he noticed she was wearing a pair of old wellies. "And having to manage you lot," she went on. "Honestly, Unwitchers can be as bad as a herd of demonically possessed ducks squabbling over a slice of blood loaf."

"It's actually a brace of ducks, unless of course they're on water, then it's a…"

"Oh shut up. Shut up and listen."

Jack tucked his chin down into his scarf.

"You made a fool of yourself and of the Guild. It's thanks to you and your histrionic, ridiculous and impertinent actions that…"

"It was a party! Did you see the way the Green Man Society was behaving? Did you hear what they said to the daughter of the Lord Chief Shaman? Shocking!"

"That was you Jack! You were the one out of control. I've never seen such a display of wanton witlessness and contumelious derangement. Unwitchers receive enough disdain as it is, then at the Mystagogue Ball, of all occasions, you behave like that; it's unbelievable!"

"I'd come straight from tackling a pylon poltergeist outside Milton Keynes. I was exhausted." He cleared his throat. "And I realise now, I should have had more to eat before I started drinking. Look Zelementra, I'll apologise to the whole lot of them, but don't banish me from the Guild."

She held a hand up to silence him. "I told you to be quiet and listen. As much as you behaved like a fool, there's more to it than just your bad behaviour. There's something rotten in the Unwitcher Guild. A bad apple somewhere.

Although you can act foolishly at times, I believe on this occasion it was manipulation. I think your drink was spiked."

"What? By another Unwitcher?" For the first time Jack looked directly at Zelementra and saw the worry behind her eyes.

She nodded. "It's possible. I've had my suspicions for a while and what happened at the ball confirms it. Someone is out to make mischief. Dangerous mischief. And you're going to help me find out who it is."

"You're assuming it isn't me then? That's a relief."

Zelementra smiled faintly. "You may be a pain in the runes, but I know I can trust you. Your behaviour the other night has proved that at least. There's no way you would have behaved like that without some outside interference. Even for you it was extreme; I don't think you were fully in control of yourself."

Perturbed, Jack pulled the scarf from his neck. "I knew it just didn't feel right, but I was expecting you to zap me into the Void for it or, at the very least, put me behind a desk at our Doncaster offices."

"No. I'm not going to do that. I'm sending you to the East Midlands. Mercia Quadrant Five."

"Quadrant Five! That's in the middle of nowhere!" he protested. "Isn't it?"

"Just outside the market town of Hexhorn. I need the other Unwitchers to think I have punished you sufficiently. You need to disappear for a while. Lay low."

"Hexhorn? Is that even a real place?"

Zelementra fished in one of her large coat pockets and pulled out a small piece of paper. "Here's the address. You're going to be living in an old Nissen hut on a farm. It's run by a friend – Mrs Ross. She's expecting you."

With indignation Jack stood up from the bench. "Surely there's something more I can be doing?"

"Sit down," Zelementra commanded. Her Unwitcher sat. "For now, I need you to do nothing. Lay low. You will hear from me."

"When?"

"When the time is right."

Jack scuffed his boot on the bare dirt. "So that's it? And now, I suppose, you're just going to disappear again in a puff of glitter."

She touched his arm gently. "Let me investigate what is going on. Someone is trying to disrupt the Unwitcher Guild. As soon as I know more, you will hear from me. Keeping out of the way is what I need you to do. For now."

He sighed. "Fine."

"There's a bus stop about a mile that way on the main road. There's a bus that can take you to Kings Lynn. You can work it out from there."

"Of course."

Zelementra stood and took a step from the bench. She turned to face Jack and raised her arms out at her sides. The wind seemed to fall silent for a moment. Just as a smile appeared upon her face there was a crackle and she vanished, leaving behind a cloud of sparks that gradually faded until there was only the scent of her perfume remaining.

Jack thought about everything his boss had just told him and listened to the anxious sea somewhere below. Wearily, he got up and began walking back along the path. "Right. So. Another exciting adventure begins. Brilliant!"

***

When Becky Bowskill arrived at Hexhorn's marketplace there were no other cars parked up, just a council van, with its engine idling whilst a man in hi-vis trousers and jacket emptied the litter bins. She parked opposite the chemists, feeling nervous. After switching off her engine she tapped the air freshener that hung over her rear-view mirror, in the hope that its aroma of Coastal Breeze might calm her, but it had lost its scent months ago and only smelt of cardboard.

Picking up her voice recorder, she took a breath and pressed its red button. "Right. I've just parked and it's 5.45am by the clock on the dashboard, which is an hour and twenty-five minutes slow, so it's actually 7.05am. Shit – and I've just realised I've left my notepad on the kitchen table. Bugger." She slapped her forehead. "Never mind. I'm due to meet Jeff Pearce at the Pop-In Café in the marketplace in Hexhorn. I've left a note explaining this, also on the kitchen table, for someone to find in case he turns out to be a proper weirdo, which I'm sure he isn't. Anyway, I'm already five minutes late, so here I go." She clicked off the recorder.

Like all good greasy spoons, the Pop-In had tables with PVC gingham tablecloths, local radio playing from a portable stereo behind the counter, and the warm fug of fried food hanging over everything. On the walls were faded photographs of Hexhorn marketplace in the 1970s. In the photos it looked somehow the same, but somehow different.

A woman, in a ketchup-stained tabard, walked over and plonked a plate in front of Jeff Pearce with the simple report, 'full English.' He nodded and immediately unsheathed his knife and fork from their napkin.

"Didn't think you'd show up. Thanks for the breakfast," he said to Becky who sat opposite with a mug of tea.

"It's really not a problem," she replied.

"Aren't you going to order something? Their bacon sarnies are bloody good."

She picked up her pen. "Er no, I'm actually vegetarian. Are you happy for me to record our conversation?"

"Makes no difference to me." Jeff started eating.

"Great." She clicked the red button of the recorder. "You said when I spoke to you on the phone something had happened that no one would believe. Something terrifying?"

"That's right."

"Maybe first of all you could tell me a little about yourself, then how you came to have this experience."

"I'm not lying, you know." He stabbed at a fried egg.

"No, of course. I'm just after a bit of background, Mr Pearce."

"Call me Jeff."

"With anyone I talk to, Jeff, I start out from the premise that they are sincere about what they tell me and so therefore, it is true. More or less."

"I see." He popped a piece of black pudding in his mouth.

"To be honest, you're the first person that's gotten in touch. I'm just starting out with all this; interviews and recording and such."

Jeff nodded. "Is that why you're writing notes in the back of a Haines manual for a 1982 Volkswagen Polo?"

Becky winced. She turned to see if any of the other patrons were paying attention to them. No one was. "Please just tell me a bit about yourself and what actually happened to you."

He took a slurp of tea and thought for a moment. "Well, my name's Jeff, a Capricorn, if that helps, and I used to be a banker in London. I jacked that in a few years ago."

"Why was that?"

"There was the crash in 08, and after that I started drinking pretty heavy. Had a sort of breakdown. Eventually I decided to get away from the city and get back to something true. I'd grown up round here you see. With what money I had, I moved back and bought a Land Rover which I sort of live in most of the time these days. I get by with a few odd jobs here and there. I've got all I need to be happy enough."

Becky reassessed the wiry and dishevelled man in front of her and tried to picture him in a suit and tie and not a jumper with holes and an army jacket. He took another mouthful of tea then got back to work on his breakfast.

"Ok. So, tell me what happened last week?" she said with her pen poised.

"As I say, I live in my Landy a lot of the time. At night I usually find a quiet lane and park up. I use a few spots – car parks are never safe and there's often the risk of doggers and boy racers."

"Of course."

"I know a lot of back roads."

"And it was at such a spot that you saw…"

"I don't know what it was. Part animal. Part demon." Jeff sat back and rubbed the grease from his moustache.

Becky looked at her recorder to make sure it was running. "Demon?"

"It came from out of the trees. Almost running, but not quite. At first, I thought it was a deer but then I realised it was stood upright, on two legs. It was humanoid but with a pair of antlers. Its skin I couldn't tell, other than it was dark. Maybe fur. It glinted in the moonlight."

"What did you do?"

"I froze. The thing came toward the Landy. It started pushing at it with its antlers. I could hear it growling and sniffing the air. Then I saw its face." He stared intently at Becky, but he didn't see her, he was seeing the beast.

"What did it look like?"

"It was the eyes. They were human eyes, like a human who has lost his soul."

All Becky had managed to write in the car manual was the word: Demon. Now she added an exclamation. Then a question mark.

"I swear to you there is a beast out there, roaming the woods and the fields. I'm going back. Tonight. Come with me. If it returns you will see it for yourself."

"Tonight?"

"There's still a three-quarter moon and the sky should be clear."

"I'm supposed to be going to Zumba with Laura tonight."

"I thought you wanted to explore this stuff. That's what your flyer said. That's why I got in touch."

Becky closed the manual. "I do. I want to explore. I'll make up an excuse. Laura's not that keen anyway."

"Tonight then? We can meet in the marketplace and I'll drive us to the spot."

"Right. Yes. No problem." The smell of fried food suddenly began to make Becky feel nauseous. She took a big swig of her tea.

"Bring a flask." Jeff told her.

She nodded.

"And put something strong in it. We'll be glad of it."

**

Becky spent the day moving between emotions. In one moment, it was excitement, the next it tipped into anxiety, pushed by questions like; what are you doing, driving into nowhere with a strange man? How will you cope with coming face to face with a demon? Do demons even really exist?

By lunchtime her boss, Graham Colby, could see that she was distracted and agitated about something. He thought that if she wanted to get a head start on the following week's audit for both the service station and vehicle sales for Colby's Garage, then it might help to refocus her. He was right and an afternoon of spreadsheets did have a mildly sedative effect.

By eight that evening she was back in the marketplace, dressed in warm, outdoor gear and with a backpack that contained a thermos flask and this time, her notebook. Jeff appeared in his battered green Land Rover. "How do," he said as she got in to the warm, rattling machine and then off they drove, into the darkness of farmland and backroads. He took them to the location of his previous encounter with the strange creature, all the while reassuring Becky. "I'll be ready this time. If that thing returns, I'm ready for it."

They parked, the engine fell silent, and the waiting began. It wasn't long before Becky's eyes began to grow heavy.

"What's the time?" she said, jolting from the sleep that had gradually crept up on her.

"Just after midnight." Jeff's eyes remained fixed on the windscreen. "I think it's time we had that coffee you brought."

Becky stirred and took the flask from her bag. "Here, I don't want any. I should keep a clear head."

"Suit yourself."

"What time are we staying until? It's just that my boss wants me to go in early tomorrow and…"

"Urgh!" he spat a mouthful of liquid over the steering wheel. "That's bloody awful! What did you put in it?"

"Coffee, and Rhubarb gin. It was all I had, and you said you wanted something hard."

"I meant whiskey or rum." The whiskers of his beard and even his eyebrows had droplets of coffee peppered over them.

"I've got some napkins in my bag," she told him.

"Sshh. Did you hear that?"

They both froze.

The noise repeated. From outside there was a low sort of grumbling which turned to a growl.

"Look!" Becky grabbed Jeff's arm.
"Something's stood at the edge of the field."

"I told you! It's looking this way. My god. The thing must be nearly ten feet. Do you see its antlers?"

"It's looking at us Jeff! Oh my god. Jeff. What should we do?"

Jeff reached behind and from underneath a blanket, produced a shotgun. "Get out and be ready to run. It's not getting away this time."

She tumbled from the Land Rover, falling face down into a patch of mud and rotten leaves. Becky did not register the cold, only the smell of the earth and the noise of the beast. It was moving closer. Once back on her feet she saw that Jeff was standing between the beams of the headlights, walking steadily into the dark, toward the creature.

"Maybe you should get out of here," he told her, raising the shotgun.

Before she could answer, the beast had leapt into the light and was all snarls and steam and coiled energy and Jeff was nothing but a twig in front of it. There was something animal and not animal about the beast. It seemed to flicker, for just a moment, from a thing with heat and mud and fur to nothing but a silhouette of red, a shape that glowed rouge like stained glass and then, in the next instant, the beast with its breath and teeth and antlers was back. Becky couldn't fathom what she saw but the twist in her stomach, and the sensation born from a deep and ancient part of her brain, told her to be truly afraid. She ran. She turned and ran and even when she heard Jeff scream, she did not stop running. It was into darkness she ran.

***

Becky opened her eyes and found a black rabbit was staring at her. It sat atop an old trunk splattered with blotches of paint of varying colours, all long since dried. The rabbit blinked, an ear twitched and then it hopped off the trunk and away into the shadows. Becky realised that a blanket had been placed over her – a coarse, grey thing that smelt the way her grandfather's workshop used to smell. Was she in some sort of a workshop now? Looking down she saw that she was sitting on a sofa patterned with faded roses and there were cushions patterned with other flowers she couldn't name. It wasn't panic or fear she felt – just disorientation.

"Becky," said a voice from the shadows. "You are safe, and no harm will come to you here." It was male and hesitant.

"How do you know my name?" she asked and was surprised at the sound of her own voice in an unfamiliar space.

"I know that you've had quite a traumatic experience tonight. I think I might be able to help you."

"Where am I?" she said standing up.

From a doorway, a figure emerged. "I'm going to turn the light on," the voice told her. "It will be bright."

Before Becky could answer, a cord was pulled and there was a metallic click as above her, a fluorescent tube flickered into life.

It was some sort of barn, was all Becky could fathom, and the man standing in front of her appeared to be living in it. From a quick glance about she could see a kitchen area and a wood burner and shelves full of junk.

"I heard a gun blast from the direction of the woods," the man went on. "I went to investigate and found you at the bottom of the track. You had collapsed."

"A gun blast?" she repeated and remembered Jeff walking toward the beast.

"Yes. We may still be able to help Jeff but will need to act swiftly."

Becky looked at the figure in front of her. The man fitted his surroundings; scruffy black hair, turning to grey, and an unkempt moustache sat above his lip like a sleeping rodent. He wore a navy-blue jumper which looked to have been repaired a good many more times than it was worth. She tried to appear undaunted by the situation and threw off the blanket still clutched about her. "We need to call the police," she said firmly. "There's a wild animal on the loose, and I need to get back to Hexhorn. I have work in the morning. I don't even know what time it is."

"Nearly two a.m. Look, Becky, I know you've had a traumatic night." He stepped toward her from the doorway. "My name is Jack Baxter, and you are safe with me, but I need you to show me where you saw this beast."

"How do you know so much? You know my name, you know about Jeff, and the animal. I think I really ought to call the police. They need to know what's happened."

"You had a bag with a recording device in it. I thought I should play it to learn something about how you came to be on the track." Jack smiled. "I must say, what you're doing is very interesting."

"Where's my phone?" Becky now felt her pockets.

"I'm afraid there was no phone on your person. I put your bag on the table," he gestured toward another dark corner of the barn where a large oak table stood. "There's no telephone here either – unless you want to wake Mrs Ross in the farmhouse, but I wouldn't advise it. She is ill-tempered at the best of times."

"Are you a farmer?" She felt utterly confused.

"There isn't time to explain now. Can you take me to where you saw this creature? Can you face that again?"

"I think so," Becky said deciding there wasn't much else to say.

"Excellent!" Jack smiled with a sudden excitement. "I have a torch ready. Let's go."

Moments later their two pairs of footsteps were walking at pace along the dirt track, the torch beam creating a holographic undergrowth around them, as if a black and white movie had been spliced onto the darkness. Jack said very little – at least to Becky. To himself he was constantly mumbling but Becky could not make out what he was saying. Her thoughts kept returning to the creature she had seen and so, to distract her mind from it, she thought about going in to work and having to pretend none of this had happened. Yes, everything is fine. Smile. She found some comfort in the anxiety this induced.

"There!" With a whispered shout Jack pointed ahead of them where the track merged with a lane. The Land Rover was there, its lights still on, the passenger door still open. With even greater alertness they stepped toward it.

While Jack stalked the area, Becky checked inside. Her phone was in the footwell. No missed calls and no messages. Typical, she thought.

"I'm picking up some strong residual displacement tones." Jack had taken something from his coat pocket. To Becky it looked like an old portable radio, though its aerial glowed different colours.

"What is that?" she asked as Jack twiddled a knob.

"An Astral Hexatic Compass. A useful tool though many consider it unfashionable these days."

"I don't understand?"

"You don't need to." Jack turned away and pointed his compass toward the fields. The aerial changed its colour again.

"Look," Becky pointed to the ground. "Jeff's shotgun." She looked closer. "It's covered in blood."

"Yes." Jack moved toward it. "And do you see – boot prints in the mud. Surrounded by…"

"They're hoof prints, aren't they? It must be a stag. It must be rutting season and this one is full of too much testosterone." Becky saw the compass aerial turn red.

"It's no stag! And it isn't rutting season. I believe Jeff fought a demon here. Look how they struggled. He put up a valiant fight."

"I'm sorry?" Becky laughed. "You seriously think it is a demon?"

"I'm afraid so. But fairly low level. From the smell I would say it was a Kastrian of some kind."

"What smell? How on earth do you know all this? I mean, I thought Jeff was a little strange, but you! You're off the charts."

Jack looked at Becky and switched his compass off. "Such a typical response." The gadget went back into his coat pocket. "Maybe you are the anomaly here. After all, in your voice recordings, you said you hardly knew Jeff."

"That's true!"

He shook his head. "Yet you got into a car with him, late at night. Why take such a risk? Wasn't it because this *strange* man claimed to have seen some sort of a beast or demon? You were prepared to believe it then. You were prepared to investigate. And why not? What else is there on a Tuesday night, aside from Zumba?"

"That's not it," Becky protested.

"Yet now, when it really counts, you're just like everybody else. You tell yourself it is nothing but a stag in the mood for romance. What nonsense!"

"I'm just trying to make sense of everything. It's been a very distressing night!"

From the darkness came a low growl followed by a grunt and a snort.

Jack turned in the direction of the sound. "The Kastrian is back. And this time it's coming for us!"

Becky grabbed hold of his arm. "What about Jeff?"

"It's too late for Jeff. It has a taste for humans now!"

A creature emerged ahead of them. It was the same beast from before. The features of it were like nothing Becky had seen – at least nothing living. The closest approximation to the creature in front of them was something like a gargoyle, like one of the stone grotesques she had often gazed up at on the side of Saint Hubert's in Hexhorn. It was a creature not of this earth. It snarled again.

"Hold this." Jack thrust the torch into Becky's hand. He unbuttoned his duffle coat and threw it to the ground.

"Are you going to use Jeff's shotgun?" Becky looked at it, covered in blood.

"No. A shotgun is ineffectual against a demon. You should turn away."

The demon cried out once more and began charging toward them, its hooves thumping on the ground.

"What are you going to do?" The torch shook in her hand.

"I'm going to urinate."

"What?"

"I told you to turn away. I won't be able to go if you're looking."

"It's getting closer!"

His zip was down, and a great arc of urine was suddenly spraying on to the mud. "No demon," he said over the thudding of the approaching monster, "especially a Kastrian demon, can stand the spicy aroma of hot, fresh Unwitcher piss. Soon as that thing is in range, watch what happens!"

"You told me to turn away!" Becky screamed.

"Here it comes!"

Just as the demon was about to leap, it stopped and snorted and reared back, away from the small moat of urine which Jack had created. The look on the creature's face changed from rage to fear, its entire form starting to shudder. Becky turned and saw. Jack was grinning, and the demon was trembling and bucking. The air was suddenly filled with a terrible smell – the odour of sulphur and decay. The beast fell to the ground as if wounded and its whole body seemed to flicker red, then disappeared with a fizz which left nothing but a cloud of scarlet fog behind to slowly dissipate in the dark.

"It has been banished!'" Jack announced triumphantly.

"But?"

"At least for the time being," he added, picking up his coat.

"What about Jeff? What about calling the RSPCA or something? I have to go to work in the morning." Becky felt unusual again.

Jack nodded as if he understood. "It has been a very eventful evening," he said, taking the torch from her and guiding her away from the scene. "Let's walk back along the track and I'll make us both a drink and we'll sit by the fire, and we can talk about everything."

"I think that might be a good idea," Becky nodded. "I don't think I've understood any of this. I might be in shock or something."

"I dare say you are. Everything will be fine."

***

The stove burned a Halloween orange and Becky was sat, once again, on the floral-patterned sofa. She now saw that the space wasn't a draughty old barn, but rather, it was more of a warm, safe den. Jack brought over two mugs of tea and placed them on top of the old trunk he used as a coffee table.

"It's incredible that you've managed to make this place so cosy. Is this some Air BnB thing?" Becky asked.

Jack sat down in an armchair opposite. "I don't know what you're talking about, but I fixed it up myself if that's what you mean. There was a tractor parked in here when I first arrived."

"How long have you been here?"

"Nearly six damn weeks."

They both sipped their tea, each waiting for the other to speak. Jack knew that certain cards would now need to be laid upon the table. He knew Becky had questions.

"Wasn't there a black rabbit here earlier?"

That wasn't one of the questions Jack had expected. "Yes," he nodded. "His name is Fletcher. He's a wild rabbit. After I arrived, he just appeared and seemed to take an interest in what I was going to do with the place. I'm not sure if he felt it was his space and I was invading it? I made the mistake of giving him a bit of food and now he seems to turn up most days. He likes sitting by the fire."

Becky put her mug down. "Who are you, Jack? The way you dealt with that thing tonight – you said demons don't like witch piss. Just what the hell does that mean?"

"Biscuit?" Jack remembered he had left a packet of custard creams by the kettle and got up to fetch it. "I realise what has occurred tonight is unorthodox and extraordinary and I will do my best to explain it." He put the packet of biscuits on the trunk and sat back down. "But I have some questions of my own," he added.

"Right?"

"I've heard your voice recordings, so I understand what you were doing tonight, with Jeff. What I need to know though, is *why* were you doing it."

"It's stupid." She took a biscuit.

Jack raised an eyebrow. "Go on?"

"I've started a blog. It's just this silly website where I investigate ghosts and the paranormal and strange stuff." She tried to read Jack's face. "It's called Becky's Macabre Cavern." She felt embarrassed.

"I see."

"Yep."

"You investigate the occult and the like?"

She nodded. "I've always liked that stuff. I split up with my boyfriend about three months ago and, y'know, I thought I'd start this blog - like a hobby. He always thought it was childish and daft."

"The man sounds like a fool. There is nothing silly or daft about the world of the paranormal, I can assure you."

Becky put her mug down. 'Ok Mr Baxter. So, who are you then? What do you know about the paranormal?"

"Yes." He suddenly noticed Fletcher sat underneath the kitchen table, staring at him, as if he were there to make sure Jack did, indeed, explain things. Jack nodded at the rabbit. "Well, Becky," he brushed his moustache. "I suppose in some way I'm like you – although I'm not a blogger. I'm what is referred to as an Unwitcher."

"And what is that exactly?"

"I'm about to tell you!" He cleared his throat. "Unwitchers have been around for many centuries, for as long as man has been curious to understand the world of the arcane and the magical."

"So, you're a magician?"

He shook his head. "On the contrary! We are often engaged to clean up problems caused by misguided or incompetent magicians – and I don't mean stage magicians either. Unwitchers are like watchmen, guarding the veil which separates this world from the realms of mysticism and witchery."

Becky thought for a moment. "How come I've never heard of Unwitchers?"

"An Unwitcher is a shadow on a summer's day, a distant dog barking, a blind spot in the corner of your eye! Our venerable and ancient institution, the Guild of Unwitchers, have always quietly protected this world from those dark realms where only malignant energies reside. We have never sought fame or notoriety."

"Unwitchers? Seriously?"

"Of course."

"So that thing we saw tonight?"

"The Kastrian demon?"

"What is it? Where has it come from?"

Jack took another biscuit and dipped it in his tea. "A low-level demonic cryptid, an untethered beast which, for some reason, is roaming free in our world. As you saw, they are easy enough to banish."

"Banish where?"

"Back to its own realm. The more important question though, is what was it doing here in the first place."

Becky nodded. "So, what was it doing here?"

"I don't know, but it's a bad sign. The veil between worlds seems to be fluttering. Kastrian demons shouldn't just be floating about like that. Something is awry."

They both fell silent. Fletcher hopped on to the trunk as if to show his solidarity, but also to nibble on a biscuit crumb.

"What do we do now?" Becky asked.

"We? We do nothing. It is my responsibility. Your involvement should not have occurred."

"But it has occurred!" The rabbit leapt on to her lap. "I can help. I'm another pair of hands and I'm into the paranormal."

"No."

"I could be a witcher too!"

Jack slumped in his chair and sighed. "It's Unwitcher. UN-WITCHER!"

Part 2:

Know Your Mushrooms

Becky Bowskill's 1982 Volkswagen Polo carefully chugged its way along the dirt track. Jack heard it coming and went into the yard to meet her.

"Hello Jack," she said, clambering out.

"Go away" he told her. "I'm busy."

Becky ignored the fact that he was wearing a dressing gown and slippers despite it being the afternoon. "Have you seen this?" she asked, waving the newspaper that was in her hand.

"Don't start reading my star sign again. I told you yesterday…"

She turned to page two. "The police have discovered Jeff's Land Rover."

"Really?" He tugged the cord on his dressing gown a little tighter. "I'll bet they haven't found Jeff."

She laid the paper on the bonnet of her car for Jack to see. "No, it says the police have discovered the abandoned vehicle of local man, Jeff Pearce, not far from the area of Scaraby Woods."

"And it makes no mention of anyone else or any strange animals?"

"Just that they are concerned for his mental wellbeing and anyone with any information should contact Hexhorn police. Do you think we should do something?"

"Absolutely not! An Unwitcher's actions can have far reaching consequences. The first thing you learn as an Unwitcher is to do the bare minimum. And never speak with the authorities. Ever."

She folded the newspaper back up. "With all the advice it sounds like my Unwitcher training has begun."

Jack shook his head. "Becky, you work in the office of a garage and petrol station."

"It's a convenience store too." As she said this, she took the newspaper and stuffed it down the front of his gown. "There's actually a lot of paperwork involved."

"The point I'm making is that your Unwitcher training has not begun and will not begin. Training to be an Unwitcher is not like going to night school. It is not something to be fitted in around a day job! It demands everything from you!"

Becky considered this. "Is that why you're hiding out in the middle of nowhere and nap most afternoons? What happened – did you get burnt out?"

Jack turned back toward the barn. "I cannot discuss that with you."

"Well, I think you're bored."

"An Unwitcher does not get bored."

She shook her head at him. "I've got something you might find interesting. It's the reason I'm here."

Jack stopped with a sigh. "What is it?"

"Kevin, one of the mechanics where I work, says he's worried about his mate Terry."

"If this has anything to do with Ouija boards then no, I'm not interested."

"Just listen. According to Kev, Terry lives an ultra-healthy lifestyle, you know – no alcohol or caffeine, lives on smoothies, lentils and meditation but for some reason, last week Terry took magic mushrooms. Just like that, out of the blue, completely out of character, and these mushrooms had some particularly weird effects."

"What on earth did Terry think would happen?"

"There's just something not right about it. Kev said that Terry reported seeing, amongst other things, a large demon with antlers – part human, part stag."

"A Kastrian demon?"

"Exactly! Sounds like it doesn't it? I have Terry's address."

Jack began marching toward Becky's car, then realised he was still in his slippers and gown. "Just give me a moment."

"I'll do the crossword," she told him, retrieving the newspaper.

***

They pulled up outside a pleasant looking detached bungalow on the outskirts of Hexhorn.

"What was his name?" Jack asked, looking up and down the road. There was no one on the street.

"Terry Thornley."

"And you've never met him?"

"No. So we're just going to knock on his door and ask him about his mushroom trip, are we?"

"I often find the direct approach works best."

They got out of the car and walked up the driveway. Becky pressed the doorbell, and it played a shrill tune. "Gosh – isn't that Eye Of The Tiger?"

Jack pulled a face. "I have no idea. Just be vigilant for anything out of the ordinary. Anything not quite right."

"Well, the doorbell for starters!"

There was a sound of movement from within the bungalow and a moment later the door opened enough for Terry Thornley to peer out. "Yes?"

Becky smiled. "Hello! It's Terry, isn't it?"

His eyes looked tired. "What's this about?"

"We have a mutual friend; Kev, the mechanic?"

"Right?"

"I'm Jack and this is Becky," Jack said, stepping forward. "We know you've recently had some magic mushrooms and we want to talk to you about it." Jack fixed his foot at the bottom of the door.

"Now wait a minute!"

"C'mon Terry." Jack pushed his weight further into Terry's doorway. "We know you went full potato on the shroom juice. You've ginsberged the badger."

"Yeah!" Becky stepped forward too. "You licked the purple spoon, didn't you!"

Terry tried to shut the door on them. "Please, just leave me alone. I don't want to talk to you."

Jack shoved himself forward. "That just isn't going to be possible. In we go!"

In a moment they were in his kitchen and Terry was following after them. "Look, I don't know what you've been told. Kev ought to keep his mouth shut. I don't want to talk to either of you."

Jack took out his Astral Hexatic Compass. "Do you have any of the mushrooms left?" he asked.

"No!"

Becky sat down at the breakfast table. "You can't lie to him Terry. He'll find out eventually so you might as well tell us what happened. Why'd you take the mushrooms?"

Terry looked at the two interlopers. Jack was holding the compass toward the fridge. "What's that thing he's got there?"

"That thing is an Astral Heptagonal Compass, isn't it Jack?"

Jack frowned. "Close enough. It's giving me some very strange readings. I'd say there's still some mushrooms here and there's something odd about them."

"I'll call the police," Terry declared.

"Do you really think that's a good idea?" Jack said, opening the fridge door, peering in, then closing it again.

"You must leave!"

"We want to help you Terry," Becky tried to sound more soothing while Jack continued to wave the compass about.

"All right, all right." Terry sat down. "They're in the protein shake tub," he told them, pointing to the worktop.

Jack investigated.

"So, what happened Terry? Kev said taking psychedelics is completely out of character for you. What made you do it?" Becky continued her soothing tone.

Terry hung his head. "I didn't even want to. It was the voices. They told me to. I know it sounds mad but it's true. I feel like I've been possessed."

Jack put the lid back on the protein tub and placed it on the table in front of Becky and Terry. "They are not your typical psilocybin mushrooms. The compass is giving me some very unusual readings and on top of that, they're neon purple with bright yellow spots."

Becky carefully opened the lid and had a look. "Gosh! Do you know what they are?"

Jack lent against the worktop. "Yes, I do. Those things are Black Magic Mushrooms. Anyone taking those things is going to find themselves being assaulted by some pretty freaky experiences."

"It's true," Terry nodded, his face pale.

"Start from the beginning," Jack advised. "How did you come into contact with these mushrooms?"

"Running," he told them. "I run three or four times a week, usually the same route along the edge of Scaraby Woods."

"And that's where you saw them?" Becky asked with a glance toward Jack. "By the woods?"

"Yes. I stopped for a moment to catch my breath by the Hangman's Oak. There it was: a patch of these mushrooms. They glowed and hummed with this wonderful sound and then from out of the sound came a voice. It told me to gather the mushrooms and to take them home. It was like I was possessed. I did. I gathered them in my vest, and I ran home with them."

Terry's eyes were fixed to the protein tub in front of him. Becky was beginning to feel nervous. "What happened next? Terry, what did you do when you got home?"

"The voice wouldn't stop. It was so powerful, so beautiful. It told me to eat. Eat the mushrooms, eat the mushrooms. Over and over, it told me. So, I did. I ate the mushrooms."

Jack shook his head. "And that's when things got fruity."

Terry looked desperately from Jack to Becky. "You need to leave. Get away from me. Now!"

Becky slowly pushed her chair away from the table. "Terry? When did you last have any of the mushroom?"

Terry's face had changed. Becky couldn't say for certain – the skin a touch redder perhaps? But his eyes! They had suddenly turned entirely yellow, so that he no longer had pupils, and his body began twitching. "What's happening to him? What's wrong with his face?"

Jack didn't need his Astral Hexatic Compass to tell him what was about to happen. "He's going to start tripping on Black Magic Mushrooms," he told her.

"What do we do?"

"Good question. The last time I saw this happen was at a black mass and craft fair just outside Hebden Bridge. It took three Unwitchers to sort out. Very bad."

Terry had stood and was stumbling toward a set of weights he kept in the corner. His yellow eyes seemed to have an expression of glee. "You can't stop it!" he told them in a maniacal voice. "It's too late for you. For all of you!"

Becky and Jack backed away. "Why don't you just put the dumbbell down?" Becky suggested.

The heavy metal weight sailed past Jack's head and thudded into a cupboard door.

"I am chaos," Terry went on in a guttural voice. "I am here to cause pandemonium!"

"No Terry! Not the medicine ball," Jack managed, before a medicine ball thudded into his stomach, knocking him backwards and on to the floor.

"No Unwitcher is going to stop this!" Terry laughed.

Becky went to Jack's aid. "We've got a problem."

Jack took in a deep breath and sat up. "Yes."

"So, what do we do?" Becky glanced back to Terry and saw he was about to grab another dumbbell.

"The only solution is that we have to destroy the source of the black magic."

"You mean, where the mushrooms came from?"

The dumbbell flew across the kitchen and clanged onto the linoleum next to where they were crouched.

"You have to go to where Terry found those mushrooms and you've got to destroy every one you find," Jack told Becky.

"Me?"

"You know the area far better than I do."

Becky thought. "He said it was near the Hangman's Oak. Everyone knows the spot; there's a clearing with a crooked oak tree in the middle."

Jack stood up. "See, you'll find the place much quicker than I would. Get some vinegar. I have a tub of it back at my place. Trample on the mushrooms and pour vinegar all over."

"I can do that. What are you going to do?"

A large inflatable balance ball struck Jack on the head and bounced off toward the living room. "I'm going to keep Terry company and make sure he stays here. He's possessed by something powerful that shouldn't be allowed to get out into this world."

"But Terry could be like this for hours, couldn't he?"

Jack smiled. "A good Unwitcher knows how to bob and weave. As soon as you have destroyed the source of the mushrooms it should break the spell and bring Terry back to normal."

Terry had begun arguing with a framed picture of Rocky Balboa.

"Just get back here as soon as you can," Jack told Becky more pleadingly.

"Right. No problem."

"And be careful. The mushrooms may try and communicate with you. Ignore them. Just do what you have to do."

***

With Jack's warning still troubling her, Becky made her way into Scaraby Woods and headed toward the Hangman's Oak. It wasn't long before she came across a large patch of mushrooms – they were purple in colour and appeared to be shimmering brightly.

"Stay back!" a chorus of high-pitched voices ordered from the ground near her feet.

Becky looked down at the glowing fungi. "You *can* talk! And you can see me too?"

All the voices made a tutting sound. "And humans consider themselves to be the dominant form of life. Ha!"

"Your colours are amazing…so beautiful." Becky was fixed to the spot, looking down at the mushroom patch as it rippled from violet to plum to mauve then magenta and back to violet.

"Yes, we are exquisite. We are unlike anything you have ever known. Why don't you taste us? Only the smallest lick and we will make you feel more wonderful than you have ever felt before. Go on."

Becky shook herself. "Got to stay focused. A good Unwitcher would stay focused in this situation."

"Pah!" came the response from the mushroom collective. "Unwitchers are all losers. No one likes Unwitchers. Haven't you noticed they spoil everybody's fun!"

Becky felt her mind beginning to float again. "Well…"

"I bet Jack Baxter treats you like a fool, doesn't he?"

"No!"

"And he doesn't let you in on all his Unwitcher secrets, does he? Well, I wouldn't worry – they're not worth knowing. Unwitchers aren't like us fungi. We're very cool. We can expand your mind. Go on, have a lick. You won't regret it."

Becky sat down crossed legged next to the patch of purple. She took the bag from her back, allowing the light-headedness she felt to wash over her. "How do you know so much about Jack?" she asked the mushrooms.

"From our master," they chorused. "Our master knows everything."

"Your master?"

"Yes. Gravestone Sam. We'll tell you all about Gravestone Sam. Just give us a lick."

Becky smiled. "And you're black magic mushrooms aren't you?"

"We are! The most exotic and fantastical fungi you will have ever experienced."

"You are superior?"

"Oh yes! We are mind alteringly superior."

Becky opened her bag. "But you're still just mushrooms, and you can't actually move, can you? Bit of a flaw in your superiority I'd say." From her bag she pulled a large plastic tub. "Here, have some vinegar." She began to pour it all over the ground.

The mushrooms cried out. "No! You fool! You stupid human fool. We're melting. Melting!"

"I've had more tempting fungi under my big toe than you lot," she told them as she continued to pour.

***

When Becky returned to Terry's bungalow, she opened the front door quietly and carefully, fearful of the scene she might be presented with. The fact that there were no concerned neighbours stood out the front and no police cars or crime scene tape gave her some comfort, but not much. Inside Terry's dojo all was quiet.

"Jack," she whispered. "Are you there?" She crept through to the kitchen and living room. "Jack?"

He was sitting on the sofa, flicking through a magazine. "You're back," he said looking up.

"What's going on?" Becky looked about the room.

"I'm just reading one of Terry's fitness magazines. You know, it's shocking the lengths that some people will go to get in shape. I'm not sure vanity should take such effort."

"I mean, what's happened? This place is a mess." There was devastation all about: broken pictures, broken furniture, holes in the plaster, a dumbbell in the ceiling. "Where's Terry?"

"I've run him a bath. He's finally relaxing." Jack swept a lamp shade from the sofa so that Becky could sit. She plonked herself down.

"Looks like you've had a pretty wild time."

"Terry was keen to give me a workout. Obviously, I was less keen. We argued a little and then all of a sudden, the effects of the mushrooms stopped, and Terry found himself confused as to why he was on top of me and about to shove a yoga DVD into a slot it was never designed for."

Becky winced. "So, you're ok?"

"Oh yes. It wasn't as bad as the time I wrestled a trouser-full of demonically possessed ferrets in Barnsley. You've done well today. You administered the vinegar just in time."

Becky allowed herself to relax a little. "It's the first time I've ever had a conversation with a fungus – obviously I'm not counting my ex-boyfriend."

"Did they try to get you to lick them?"

"Yes. Do you think there'll be more that appear?"

A look of worry appeared on Jack's features. "I think it very possible. There's something weird going on in Scaraby Woods."

"Jeff said he first saw the Kastrian demon on the other side of the woods to where the mushrooms were. Do you think they're linked?"

"They have to be." Jack looked into Becky's eyes and thought he understood the anxiety in them. "Don't worry," he tried to reassure. "If anyone else has tried those mushrooms they'll be ok now you've destroyed the cluster. If anyone is affected, they'll be just like Terry – exhausted but relatively normal again."

"There's something else," Becky told him. "The mushrooms knew about you, and they mentioned the name of someone. They said this person was their master."

"Who?"

"Does Gravestone Sam mean anything to you?"

Jack stood up. "Are you sure the mushrooms said Gravestone Sam?"

"I'm certain. What's wrong? Who is he?"

Jack began to pace. "Gravestone Sam is trouble. The kind of trouble that makes Kastrian demons and talking mushrooms seem like silly carnival sideshows."

Part 3:

The Magpie's Song

The marketplace was silent and still in the slowly diminishing dark. A man in a duffle coat appeared from round a corner and hurried toward an old phone box across from the post office. The man opened its heavy red door and stepped inside. He pulled the coins from his pocket and placed them on the small shelf, then removed the hood of his coat. Lifting the receiver, he dialled the number he had memorised. On the seventh or eighth ring Becky finally answered.

"Hello?" Her voice was confused and sleepy.

"I need you to come and pick me up. Please"

"Jack, is that you?" She groaned and yawned.

"Of course."

"It's half past four in the morning. What on earth are you doing?"

"An Unwitcher is always on duty Becky – I thought that would be clear by now."

She sat up, slightly more awake. "You don't have a telephone. Where are you?"

Jack sighed as if it were obvious. "A telephone box in Hexhorn marketplace."

"But that's three miles from where you live."

"Yes. I know."

"You've walked three miles and it's half past four in the morning?"

"I know you're probably half-asleep Becky, but yes, that is correct. I can explain more when you get here."

"Is this something to do with demons?"

"Get yourself a coffee and get over here. Please. I shall be waiting." He hung up and stepped back outside into the marketplace. Taking a seat on a bench, he allowed himself a moment to enjoy the quietude before the worry began to jab at him again.

Before long Becky's car arrived and Jack got in.

"I thought you'd at least have gotten dressed," he said as Becky pulled away.

"Well, I assumed it was quite urgent so I got here as soon as I could. I didn't even have coffee."

Jack looked at Becky more closely. "Your dressing gown actually matches your pyjamas. I've never seen that before – it's an impressive level of coordination."

Becky indicated her annoyance through a jerked gear change. "I don't know why I didn't just tell you to sod off and go back to sleep! I'm supposed to be at work in four hours."

"I do appreciate your help."

She glanced at her passenger. "I don't understand why Unwitchers aren't allowed to drive - seems very convenient."

"I explained this – it's one of the rules that all Unwitchers are bound by, and I find it very inconvenient much of the time."

They stopped at Hexhorn's main crossroads. The only other vehicle on the road was a tractor waiting at the opposite junction. "So, where are we going?" Becky asked.

"Take us to Low Scaraby. Specifically, its churchyard."

"The churchyard? Is this going to involve the undead or poking about in graves? Because I don't think I can do that – not in pyjamas, not even if you gave me a hazmat suit."

Jack looked at the sunrise that was emerging from behind the rolling hills. "It's nothing like that. I'm hoping we can get some information as to what exactly is going on in this quadrant."

"You mean all the demons and talking mushrooms."

"Precisely. Our recent fracas with Terry and the Black Magic Mushrooms on top of the Kastrian demon, is a pretty good barometer that something isn't right. I'm now quite concerned."

They drove in silence and the light grew stronger. After a few moments Becky asked a question. "Didn't you say there's a Guild of Unwitchers?"

"So, you do listen to me."

"Couldn't you get in touch with them? Wouldn't they know what's going on?"

"It's complicated," Jack told her. "I'd rather do it the old-fashioned way first."

"And this is the old-fashioned way?"

"Yes – we're going to speak to the magpie."

Becky shot him a look. "Go on then. Explain that."

"In every part of the land there is a magpie assigned to an Unwitcher. It has been this way with magpies ever since the devil put a spot of blood beneath the bird's tongue." Jack smiled.

"You mean an actual magpie, with feathers and a beak?"

"Yes. Unwitchers have a covenant with magpies. The magpie knows all that goes on in its territory. Should the Unwitcher call upon the bird it must inform the Unwitcher of all that it knows – but only in the hours of morning. That is why we are up so early."

"We are going to speak to your informant, which is a bird. A talking magpie?"

"Correct on all counts." He retrieved his Astral Hexatic Compass from his pocket and looked at its lights. "According to the compass and the information I took from my runes, it is the churchyard of Low Scaraby where we will find our magpie. Are we far away?"

As he asked this Becky slowed down and turned off the main road. "We'll be there in about five minutes," she told him. "The church is called Saint Bosco's. My dad was an organist, so he's played in a lot of the churches around here and dragged me along too."

"And he's played at Saint Bosco's?"

Becky nodded. "I remember he said he never much liked playing in Low Scaraby. It always gave him the willies."

"Good. It sounds like the right place."

The car continued its way along the quiet country road which began to weave on a gradual downward slope and into the village of Low Scaraby, sleepy and soundless in the five thirty morning light. Becky parked near a row of cottages across from the lychgate of the churchyard and they got out. Jack led the way, all the while staring at the wavering lights on his compass. He took a meandering course over the graves until stopping in the midst of several old headstones with Saint Bosco's ahead of them.

"So, what now?" Becky asked a little impatiently.

"This is the first time I have contacted the designated magpie. On each occasion you must call the magpie to you. If our magpie is near, then it should respond."

Becky looked around. She could see a couple of crows, a blackbird and the obligatory pigeon, but no magpie. "How do we call a magpie? Will a simple, hey magpie, do?"

"Don't be ridiculous." Jack dropped the compass back in one pocket of his duffle coat and from the other retrieved a piece of paper. "We must call the magpie with a song. It has been used by Unwitchers for centuries. I've written the words out for you."

Becky let out a little gasp. "You want me to sing it with you! That makes me feel valued. Thank you." She took the scrap of paper from him.

"You're here anyway," Jack shrugged. "Another voice can only help when it comes to calling forth an Unwitcher's magpie."

Becky looked about again to make sure no one was around to hear her.

"I'll sing it through first," Jack advised. "Then you join in the second time."

Becky nodded.

Jack cleared his throat and began:

"Ho hey magpie!

Speak with me this morning.

Ho hey magpie!

More handsome than a robin.

Ho hey magpie!

It is the morning hour.

Ho hey magpie!

Wiser than an owl."

On the second round Becky joined in, timidly to begin but Jack nodded his encouragement, and she became a little bolder. By the third go she could hear a full compliment of instruments in her head, backing her up.

"Ho hey magpie…"

"Shhh!" Jack stopped her. "Listen."

There came a fluttering sound. It was hard to pinpoint where from. The fluttering became a kawing noise and then a magpie landed atop a nearby gravestone, folded its wings and looked intently at Jack and Becky. Then it spoke.

"Argh. Who is it that calls me with the ancient song?"

"We do," Jack replied in his best authoritative voice.

"And who are you to speak with me?"

"My name is Jack Baxter. I am now the designated Unwitcher for Mercia Quadrant Five. To whom am I speaking?"

The bird gave a little hop. "Designated Unwitcher? There's been no Unwitcher in this quadrant for many a year – and now there are two standing before me!"

Jack shook his head. "No, you misunderstand. I am the Unwitcher. This is Becky. She is not an Unwitcher."

"Argh. An apprentice then. It's all the same to me."

"No. Becky is not an apprentice."

"I don't care." The bird told him.

Jack tried to steer the meeting back on track. "I have called you," he said, emphasising the 'I.' "It is the morning so you must answer my questions."

The magpie fluttered on to another headstone, closer to them. "I might have known someone would turn up eventually."

Jack could see the smirk beginning to appear on Becky's face. "Magpie!" he spoke more loudly. "What is your name?"

The bird cocked its head. "My name is Spadework. Spadework of the woods and fields here about. This is my churchyard. You have come to find out what is going on, yes?"

"So, there is something going on?"

"Oh, there is much going on Unwitcher. Your ignorance would make a fairy blush! Argh."

"Is it something to do with Gravestone Sam?" Becky interjected.

Spadework flapped. "Ha; so, your non-apprentice knows a name. What an impressive pair you make."

"Enough of the chatter, Spadework." Jack had already taken a dislike to the bird. "Tell me everything you know."

Spadework took to the air once more and came to land a little further away, on a rusted bin into which mouldy flowers had been cleared away. "Perhaps it has been too long since you conversed with a magpie, Jack. Perhaps you have forgotten some of the rules."

"I'm starting to wonder if I shouldn't just ring your neck and bake you in a pie," Jack grumbled under his breath.

Spadework went on. "On their first encounter with the designated magpie, an Unwitcher must agree to aid the magpie in a simple task, to be determined by the magpie. Once the task is completed, the magpie is solemnly bound to answer all future questions from the Unwitcher."

"Yes, well I thought we might just get on with things."

"Argh. Rules must be followed Jack."

"Can I ask?" said Becky stepping forward. "What is meant by a simple task?"

Jack sighed. "It's mostly something like bringing the magpie food or finding some twigs for its nest."

Becky checked her watch, conscious that she was at work later that morning. "Doesn't sound like that will take us too long."

The magpie gave its raspy call and leapt to the air, returning to another headstone, this one taller and grander than before. "Argh. Usually you would be correct – but on this occasion there's something else I want."

"What?" Jack asked.

"You see up there on the tower of the church. Inside one of the gargoyle mouths, the one on the right corner, there is a silver ring. I have tried to get to it, but my beak will not reach. I want you to climb up there and retrieve the ring for me."

Becky looked up at the Norman tower. "How did a ring get all the way up there?"

"I don't know, but I want it! Retrieve the ring, that is the simple task I am setting you, Jack Baxter."

"That gargoyle is a long way up," Becky declared.

"Yes," Jack agreed.

"And some of the stones and the mortar look as if they've had better days."

"Yes!"

"And, if you fall, nothing but nettles and a compost bin to break your fall."

"All right, yes! Thank you, Becky. Thank you for pointing all of that out."

"Come on!" squawked Spadework. "You don't have all morning."

For what was perhaps the first time, Becky saw a look of genuine fear appear on the face of the Unwitcher. "What's wrong, Jack?" she asked.

He turned away from the church. "I don't like heights. I never have."

"Ha!" flapped Spadework. "This is going to be interesting then."

"I'll do it," Becky told the bird.

"No! I want Jack to do it. He's the Unwitcher after all."

Jack began marching toward the church, the other two following after him. "Give me a demon or a pylon poltergeist and I'm fine, but heights! No. I hate heights."

"This is the task I'm giving you," Spadework said, gliding through the air. "If you want answers to your questions, you must get me that shiny from the mouth of the gargoyle."

Becky removed the cord from her dressing gown. "Here, take my dressing gown cord. You could use it like a rope or something."

"Thanks. If I fall, I'm sure its soft flannelette will help to cushion my landing. Here, take my coat." He took the cord and exchanged it with his duffle coat which he plonked into Becky's arms. With that he leapt on to the top of a water tank that was fixed against the corner of the church. From there he grasped at the stonework and began to climb upward.

Becky watched him heave his body higher whilst Spadework went to flutter about his head. "That's it!" the bird told him excitedly.

"Can you go away?" Jack snarled with his face squashed against the crumbling loaves of stone.

"The best thing is not to look down," Spadework told him. "Just look up at me."

"All I'm looking at is where to put my hand, thank you very much!"

It felt as if every muscle he had was beginning to wobble and lose its strength, but he could see the grinning head of the gargoyle getting closer. He had managed to climb high enough that he was just a few feet from a drainpipe which ran down from the roof of the tower.

"I'm going to grab that drainpipe," he told the others. "I can claw my way up on it."

"Be careful!" Becky called from below.

Jack stretched his arm out and just managed to touch the ironwork. He could feel the stone crumbling beneath his boots as he tried to shift his weight but then, somehow, his body seemed to know how to move and had propelled itself sideways, his arms clasped together and he was kissing the cold, metal pipe.

"Argh! You're almost there," Spadework told him from a ledge. "A little higher and you will be close enough."

Jack cursed the bird and pulled himself upwards. With a clanking groan, the drainpipe in turn cursed Jack.

"That's it," cried the magpie. "Just reach your hand in its mouth and pull out the ring!"

His entire body shook. "Yes, I bloody know! I can feel it, just trying to grab the damn thing."

"The drainpipe is coming loose!" Becky told them.

Jack did not hear her. "I've got the ring," he told the bird. "It's light as a feather? It's…it's…it's just a ring pull from a drink's can! Vimto? It says bloody Vimto on it!"

Spadework flew into the air. "I still want it!"

The drainpipe groaned with more anger as it tore away from the stonework. Jack felt everything shift and then he was tumbling and falling back to the earth.

***

He opened his eyes and felt relieved that there was no overwhelming pain in his body, just a generalised throbbing discomfort all over. "Where am I?" he asked.

Becky was at his side. "You're lying on a bench in the churchyard at Saint Bosco's. Do you want to sit up?"

"In a minute, when the wooziness stops."

"You did a marvellous fall onto that compost bin," Spadework told him enthusiastically. "It was the funniest thing I've seen in ages. Argh! The look on your face as you fell!"

"I think you should show a little more gratitude," Becky told the bird. "Jack could have really injured himself, all for a stupid ring pull."

"I don't think it's stupid. I've been after it for months."

"I'm going to sit up very slowly," Jack informed them. "Once I'm up, Spadework, you'd better start answering some questions."

"I said I would, didn't I? I'm a magpie of my word and now, from this moment forth, I shall answer you whenever you call me. I am your magpie."

Jack sat up and swung himself round, making room for Becky to sit next to him. The magpie now flew over and came to rest on her arm.

"What do you want to know?" Spadework asked.

"We want to know about Gravestone Sam," Jack replied.

"Argh! He is loathsome and twisted and now walks the earth."

Jack shook his head. "But he was banished. Zelementra herself saw to it that Gravestone Sam was trapped in the Void and would never be able to return to this realm."

"I'm sorry," Becky interrupted. "Zelementra?"

"She manages all Unwitchers," Spadework informed her. "In charge of them all."

"Some years ago," Jack went on, "Zelementra dealt with a free roaming sprite who was evil and hungry for more power. The sprite was called Gravestone Sam."

"What do you mean, free roaming?" Becky asked, worried that Jack would get frustrated with her questions, but his usual grumpiness had gone.

"Argh! Sprites are usually subservient creatures," Spadework answered. "Powerful magicians or even Unwitchers often kept them as pets or servants. Sometimes a sprite would be given its freedom and become free roaming in this realm."

"That's what happened to Gravestone Sam," Jack added, the look of worry back on his face.

"But Sam is unnaturally powerful," Spadework said grimly. "He caused havoc."

"Many Unwitchers died trying to stop him. I tried too but, in the end, it was Zelementra that faced him and won. She banished him to the Void; a place beyond this realm, a place we thought he could not return from."

"But now?" Becky felt she was beginning to understand how bad things might be.

"All I know is that Gravestone Sam is back and Zelementra has gone missing," Spadework told them.

"What?" Jack leapt from the bench. "When did this happen?"

"Argh! No one has heard from her for nearly a month."

"Zelementra sent me to live here six weeks ago! She thought there was a traitor among the Unwitchers. I have been waiting for her to contact me again."

"I have heard no rumours of a traitor. It must be Gravestone Sam. Argh!"

Jack began to pace. "What are all the Unwitchers doing about it?"

"I do not know. There has been silence for days, until you appeared this morning. All I know is that the omens are bad. Moonlight no longer shimmers on the streams and the trees sway backward in the wind."

Jack felt sick. "Why haven't I felt any of this? As soon as we saw the Kastrian demon I should have realised something was wrong."

"It's Gravestone Sam!" Spadework flew to Jack's shoulder. "He's polluting the energies everywhere. He's blocking things."

"He's taking his revenge," Jack concluded.

"We can do something about it though, can't we?" Becky stood up too now. "We can stop him from whatever he is planning."

Spadework shook his head. "Gravestone Sam is powerful and cannot be underestimated."

"How come he's so powerful?"

"He was released by his master," Jack told her. "It should not have been allowed."

"I don't understand?"

Spadework flew onto the head of a weeping angel. "Gravestone Sam's master gave him too much power and revealed too many secrets to him. Now we are all in danger."

Becky turned to Jack. "Who is it? Who is this master that set him free?"

"Argh! It was the one who causes the veil between worlds to flutter. The blackest shadow of the sun. Old Scratch. Baphomet. Beelezebub."

Becky sat back down and breathed. "You mean…?"

Jack nodded. "Gravestone Sam's master was Lucifer."

Part 4:

The Mystic Doughnut

"Good morning Zelementra. Time for breakfast."

The rickety door caught the breeze and swung shut behind the strange creature, causing the entire structure to groan and shake. Gravestone Sam carefully touched the back of his head and, satisfied his hair was not out of place, carried on. "That's right, morning all ready." He held a cup toward the woman lying on the bare concrete floor.

Zelementra shook her head. "No more. I don't want any."

Gravestone Sam pretended to be hurt. "But this Black Magic Mushroom juice is my own recipe!"

Zelementra managed to pull herself up but immediately felt dizzy. "No," was all she managed to say.

"Not only does it cloud your mind so you can't do any of that teleportation nonsense, but I've added some fibre and vitamins. Even I understand the importance of a good breakfast – I'm not a monster."

Zelementra let her head hang down. She was so muddled, so exhausted by this never-ending fever dream.

Gravestone Sam drew closer. "Well, perhaps I am a bit of a monster, but only in this realm and that won't matter for much longer. It will be full of monsters soon enough!" He pulled Zelementra's head back, ready to pour the black juice down her throat.

"You won't succeed," she told him in a whisper. "I won't allow it."

Gravestone Sam laughed. "You're tied to the engine block of an old Massey Ferguson in an abandoned gamekeeper's hut on the edge of a wood, miles from anywhere. You are not in a position to do anything."

"My Unwitchers will!"

He pulled violently on her hair, tipping her head as far back as it would go. He began to pour the black magic mushroom juice. "They tried that before, remember, but couldn't manage it. They had to send you to deal with me!"

The black slime dribbled all about Zelementra's lips and she could taste its mouldering flavour down the back of her throat. "There'll be a dozen Unwitchers on your trail," she hissed.

"It's just a matter of time." She toppled to the floor, panting and coughing up inky mucous.

"You really have no idea how pathetic you look and sound. I bet you have no idea how bad you smell too!" Gravestone Sam looked about the decaying hut and kicked at a patch of long dried pigeon faeces. It immediately crumbled and scattered across the concrete floor. "The only creatures that are going to find you will be the rats looking for another meal. There won't be any Unwitchers coming."

Zelementra tried to speak but could only groan.

"Always full of your own importance," he went on, "like a headmistress for a gang of unruly children." He stopped and adjusted his tie. "Well, I'm in charge now and the class shall soon be dismissed."

Zelementra managed to sit herself up against the chunk of metal she was tied to. She breathed heavily and recovered herself a little. "I won't believe it," she told the figure in front of her.

"It doesn't matter what you believe." Gravestone Sam touched his hair again, lightly with the palm of his small, green hand. "Your Unwitchers have indeed realised you are a prisoner, unfortunately, they think you are captive far away, in the remains of a remote Scottish castle."

"What have you done you diminutive, demented demon!"

"Whilst you have been under the influence of my mushroom juice for the last few days, I have been able to take control of your weakened mind."

"You horrid shit!"

"You have given me all your access codes," he went on. "So, I have been able to fire off a few frantic messages from you to your admin staff in Doncaster. They did all the difficult work for me – letting your Unwitchers know you are in peril and have been snatched by…" Here he paused and pretended to think, tapping a scaly finger against his cold, black lips. "Who was it? Yes, that's right – Jack Baxter, your disgraced Unwitcher. That's just the sort of thing he would do, isn't it?" Gravestone Sam leapt with glee onto an old wooden chair as if it were his stage.

Zelementra shook her head. "My Unwitchers will not believe that nonsense."

The sprite laughed. "I'm afraid they did believe it – every word of it. Your Unwitchers think you are Baxter's prisoner at Galdoun Castle in the

Highlands. I believe they're gathering themselves at Penrith to discuss how to rescue you."

"The damn fools!"

"Yes, I thought so too. By the time they have actually worked out what is happening, it will have already happened."

Zelementra looked at the short, green skinned thing in front of her, smiling pompously in a tailored suit, unaware his wig had slipped and was now sitting slightly crooked atop his bald head. She tried to channel her hatred and for a moment she felt some strength return. "What are you planning?" she managed to say in a voice stronger than before.

Gravestone Sam chuckled to himself once again. "Apart from the total elimination of you and your Guild of Unwitchers? Well, I thought I might make use of this tatty realm a little more – turn it into a sort of executive retreat for me and my friends. I'd say a demon of my calibre could do with an executive retreat."

Now Zelementra managed a laugh. "You're no demon. You're a jumped-up little sprite in a silly wig!"

Gravestone Sam hopped down from the chair then adjusted his hairpiece. "It's going to be a shame you won't be around," he said making sure his hair was back in place. "Of course, I might keep you on as a pet – you're already starting to smell like some sort of animal."

"There have been Unwitchers for a thousand years. You won't change that."

"I'll just try anyway. You've already done so much to help me, and I've got plenty of mushroom juice just for you."

Zelementra's sudden strength was already beginning to wane. She watched Gravestone Sam pick up the feeding bowl. "Don't give me any more of that."

He ignored her. "Eventually you'll lose your mind entirely – another day or two and you'll be completely fried. Then it won't be long before word spreads that the great Zelementra is no more."

"No!"

"Things will finally start to get interesting around here."

Zelementra could barely hold her head up. "Please. No more."

"There really is no choice. Open wide."

***

Jack could bear the sound no more. He turned to Becky, sat in the driver's seat next to him. "You really shouldn't bite your nails. That clicking noise is awful. I can't think."

Becky took her fingers from her mouth and instead started tapping on the steering wheel. "I don't know what's making me more anxious: having to find and destroy a power crazed demon trained by Satan himself or lying to my boss that I'm ill and won't be in today."

From the churchyard at Low Scaraby they had said goodbye to Spadework and driven back to Hexhorn and were now parked outside the library.

"So, what did your boss say when you spoke to him?"

Becky began to bite her nails again. "He reminded me we're in the middle of an audit and told me I'd better be feeling well enough tomorrow."

"If we don't find Gravestone Sam and stop him there won't be any point in going back to work. We'll all be slaves to darkness and despair."

Becky took her hands from her mouth again and looked at Jack forlornly. "That sounds very much like working in admin."

Jack sighed and looked over at the closed doors of the library. "What's the time now?"

"Nearly nine. It should be open soon."

Jack was still unconvinced by Becky's idea. "And you really think we're going to find what we need at the local library?"

"You might not think I've been paying attention, but I have."

"There was one time when I had to track down a hell hound," Jack began. "It had escaped from, well, you can guess where. The area I had to cover was vast, so I managed to commandeer a helicopter. It was Zelementra really who pulled some strings and found a pilot willing to fly. Anyway, once we were in the air the beast was located pretty quickly."

"Did you kill it?" Becky asked.

"Of course. It was a rabid dog of Hades. The point I'm trying to make is that a helicopter made all the difference. Getting some big hardware like that just isn't an option here."

"And that's why I think we should try the library."

"So, explain."

"Earlier you said you didn't understand why you hadn't picked up on Gravestone Sam being nearby."

Jack nodded. "My runes should have indicated something."

"Right!" Becky started to feel more confident. "Spadework told us that Sam has been disrupting things and blocking energies, which is why your runes didn't work."

"I realise that now."

"And I'm right in thinking that your runes can act like magnets?"

Jack frowned. "I don't use them to stick my shopping list to the fridge, no."

Becky tried again. "I mean, they're like magnets in the way they can be affected by fields. I don't know what you'd call it – psychic fields or energies? The way iron filings will line up due to magnetic fields. Like that."

"Yes. Something like that."

"So, if you were to spread your runes out over a large map of this entire area, wouldn't they indicate lines of psychic or weird energy?"

"They would." Jack began to understand.

Becky knew she was on to something now. "If Gravestone Sam is blocking things, then won't that be like a sort of black hole? Wherever that black hole is, that's where we'll find Sam."

Jack clapped his hands. "If I charge the runes correctly, they should indeed line up and form a circle. If Sam is shielding his presence, then it should appear that the circle has a gap at the centre – a hole."

"Like the centre of a mystical doughnut!"

"If you like." Jack looked toward the library. It was beginning to open "So what's in there?" he asked, nodding toward the doors.

"A huge local map in the reference section and a big table we can spread it out on. I thought it would be the best place."

"Good work Becky," he told her already opening the car door. "Let's go and discover the centre of the doughnut!"

***

The main area of the library had seen more modernisation than the reference section. Its beech shelving units were new back in the nineties and had managed to keep their freshness thanks to a regime of tireless dusting and wiping. On the walls, between community noticeboards and pastel pictures of flowers in vases, the green paint from the seventies had been hidden by a dusky pink twenty years its junior and both colours were, here and there, battling and winning against an optimistic yellow that had been applied at the turn of the twenty-first century. Orange carpet tiles of undetermined vintage did their best to pull the disparate municipal miens together.

Becky and Jack quickly marched past the comfortable armchairs and coffee table and then past the computer corner where half a dozen black PCs were still booting up and then, into the older, Victorian part of the library. Becky always felt that moving into this back room was like entering a headmaster's office – a place of dark, austere wood, the scent of polish and a feeling that time itself had decided to move at a slower, more hushed pace.

Becky knew where to find the large map and immediately pulled it from its file and unfolded it on to the large, oak table.

"As far as I know, this is the largest map of the area. Do you think it's big enough?"

"Shh," Jack whispered. "Speak a bit more quietly." He glanced back through the doorway to the main room.

"Why?"

Jack continued to whisper. "It's a library! I don't want to get thrown out – we look strange enough with you still dressed in your pyjamas. I don't even have a library card."

Becky looked at him incredulously. "What? Is that another one of your Unwitcher rules – you mustn't join a library? Honestly, it's like some sort of cult."

"Shhhh! Of course Unwitchery is not a cult. That's ridiculous!"

Becky continued to flatten out the map. "There's no need to worry. No one is around yet and I know the librarian. Trish is lovely."

"Let's just be as subtle as possible, do what we need to and then leave."

"Agreed. Have you got your runes?"

"They're not runes Becky, they're Unwitcher runes – there is a vast and important difference."

"Are all you Unwitchers like this?"

"Like what?"

"Pedantic. Let's just get on with this, shall we?"

From his coat pocket, Jack took a well-worn, small canvas bag. "I'll scatter them across the map and with luck they should form a pattern."

"A doughnut."

"Yes, if our theory…"

"My theory."

Jack put his hand in the bag and pulled out a dozen dull black stones like polished coal. On each one Becky could make out red lines and circles in a variety of configurations.

"If the theory is correct," Jack went on, "then there should be a clear energy pattern. If there is a space at the centre, Gravestone Sam and Zelementra must be the reason."

Becky nodded.

"Here goes." He tossed the black stones across the table.

The silence of the reference room seemed even louder after the runes' skittering came to a stop. Then, out of the silence a hum began, as if an electrical substation had just been switched on behind the dictionaries and encyclopaedias.

"They're moving!" Becky tried to whisper.

"Yes! They're aligning."

The humming continued low, a droning tune which seemed to follow the movement of the black pebbles across the map.

"There's a pattern!" Becky moved around the table.

"It should be easy to see where there is a hole. Hopefully it won't be too big."

"Ooh! Spoken like a typical bloke!" A woman clutching a duster appeared from round the corner.

Becky jumped. "Trish!"

The woman had a brown cardigan and a limp perm and gave a big, red lipped smile to Becky. "Don't you two mind me – I always give Local Reference and History a little dust on a Tuesday morning. I'll not hoover though as I can see you're busy."

"We're nearly done," Becky told her, then glanced at Jack. She could tell he was perturbed.

Trish didn't seem to hear. "It's the cuts you see. Won't even pay for a cleaner now. We're luckier than most. Over in Scaraby they have to double up with the Brownies and last week half the little buggers had sickness and diarrhoea. Had to throw out most of Religion & Philosophy after they'd finished. This your new fella then?"

Jack cleared his throat. "Excuse me?"

Trish stepped closer and gave his arm a little dusting. "I know I should keep my nose out. You just say, Becky. He's an improvement on the last one though love." She looked Jack up and down. "Bit more mature but there's nothing wrong with that. My Wayne's seven years older than me."

Jack tried to smile but the expression came out more like he'd wet himself.

Trish looked him in the eye. "I can tell he's the dark mysterious type."

Becky steered her away from Jack and away from the table. "We're just friends, Trish," she smiled. "He hasn't even got a library card."

Trish took her by the hand, still holding the duster. "He must be doing something for you, love. You're still in your PJs and I bloody respect that."

"Our association is professional," Jack chipped in, stiffly.

Trish turned back and gave him a wink. "It's alright, handsome. You two can do what you like. I'm forever turning a blind eye in this place – not paid enough to worry. Just as long as you treat her with a bit of kindness."

"Honestly Trish," Becky told her. "I'm usually dressed by now."

Trish walked off. "Don't worry, love. You do you. And if you've got any sense, you'll do him and all!" she let out a high-pitched chuckle. "I'll leave you to it." Before she got to the doorway she stopped and turned about. "Oh, and before I forget – that book on ghosts you ordered has come in. Right scary looking cover."

Becky breathed a sigh. "Thanks, Trish."

"No bother. You two take care." She nodded at the table with the map on it and gave another wink. "There's already enough ghouls and goblins around here. No need to read a book on it." With that she turned and was gone, saying good morning to someone who was in the main room.

Jack and Becky looked at one another. The runes had stopped their twitching and a clear hole had formed at their centre.

"I'll make a note of that shall I?" Becky asked.

Jack just nodded.

***

When they returned to Jack's barn, Fletcher, the black rabbit, was there to greet them. Once Becky had given him a little fuss he quickly disappeared into the shadows.

Becky collapsed onto the sofa. It was only mid-morning, but she felt exhausted "I don't suppose you have something I could change into? If I have to do battle with a vengeful demon, then I think it's time I got out of my nightwear."

Jack thought for a moment. "There's a boiler suit in the back."

"A boiler suit?"

"Don't worry, it's more or less clean." Jack went over to a small collection of books he had on one of the shelves.

"So, that place on the map where there were no runes – I don't think it's too big an area," Becky told him.

"What do you know about it? I thought I might try and cross-reference it with some of my books." He looked forlornly at his collection. "What I have is just so limited."

"I can tell you this," Becky stood back up for fear she would simply fall asleep if she kept sitting. "The locals call that area the Barley Triangle. Loads of unusual things are supposed to have happened around there."

"Such as?"

She shrugged. "Ghost sightings, UFOs, that sort of stuff. Low Scaraby and Hexhorn both dispute it's in their parish boundary. Neither of them wants it."

"So, it really is a black hole." Jack disappeared behind a door for a moment and returned with a boiler suit which he threw at Becky. "There you go."

She caught it and frowned at its rough cotton texture. "There isn't much of anything in the Triangle," she told him. "Apart from fields and old farm buildings."

"That's where we need to look first: old outbuildings and the like. We don't have any time to waste."

From a dark corner of the barn there was a clattering sound. Becky thought it might have been Fletcher but then the noise came again from another corner and then another corner, like an echo that seemed to be spinning about.

"Stand still," Jack commanded.

A sudden gust of wind swirled through the barn, whipping up the fine dust that had settled on all its ancient surfaces. For the second time that morning a strange humming sound began to rise, like some sort of static chant.

"Jack! What's happening?"

"Stay where you are. Something is trying to come through. A psychic presence."

"This place is going to fall down." Becky felt the atmosphere change, everything shook and then the dust seemed to coalesce and began to glow as it came together in a swirling orb.

"Look!" Jack was pointing at the light.

"Time is running out, Jack," said a distorted voice from within the swirling glow. "Sam wants to destroy us."

Becky could see the figure of an older lady. She did not look well.

"Zelementra!" Jack shouted. "We're coming for you. You must hang on."

"Listen to me," the woman demanded. "Sam has fooled everyone. They think I am at Galdoun Castle, and they are on their way to rescue me. It's a trap!"

"How many Unwitchers?" Jack asked.

The light flickered. "All of them."

"The fools!"

"Jack, listen. You must try and stop them. They think you have taken me, but you have to try and make them understand the truth."

Jack shook his head. "But we can save you. I am close by. Tell us where you are."

"I don't have long Jack. My survival is not important, but the Guild must survive, or Sam will take control of everything. You must save the Unwitchers."

The throbbing static became louder again, and the orb began to fade.

"Zelementra!" was all Jack could manage and then she was gone, and the barn creaked in the sudden silence.

Jack and Becky were left facing one another. "It was Zelementra," Jack told her.

"I know."

"They're all heading for Galdoun Castle. They think I've done this. They think I've kidnapped her."

Becky looked to where the flickering image had been. "Zelementra said not to rescue her. We can't save her and the Unwitchers as well."

He thought about how Zelementra had looked – pale, withered, fragile. "But we have to save her," he said.

"What are we going to do Jack? What are we going to do?"

Part 5:

Inside The Barley Triangle

Becky did not slow down, even as the tractor got larger and larger, its chunky rear wheels obscuring any view of the road ahead. She veered into the oncoming lane and flew past the trundling farm vehicle. The farmer had a look of surprise but not as much as the driver of the postal van, who suddenly had a Volkswagen Polo appearing ahead of him. The postie hit his brakes and the horn at the same time.

"Sorry!" Becky winced as she jolted her wheel to the left and tucked her car back in just ahead of the tractor. The post van shot past as a red blur. Becky breathed and gripped the wheel harder but did not slow her frantic speed.

Taking one hand from the wheel she reached over to the audio recorder she had put on the passenger seat. Her finger found the button and pressed it to start recording.

"I must be crazy," she began. "Jack, if you are listening to this recording at some point in the future then I should think things didn't work out quite as I'd hoped. If that's the case, I'm sorry but I thought what I'm doing was for the best.

"What am I doing?" This question had only been given a foggy answer in her mind and now her unconscious rose up to demand a fuller explanation. "I'm not on my way home to get changed out of this boiler suit, like I told you. I'm on my way to find the magpie. Jack, I know you were going to try and make a psychic connection to one of your Unwitchers and I know you didn't want to. I know what you really want to do is save Zelementra before it's too late. So that's what I'm doing!" For a moment her explanation had given her belief. "I know you wouldn't allow this but I'm trying to think like an Unwitcher. Please don't laugh. If I can speak to Spadework and convince him to help me, then maybe we can find Zelementra before it is too late. Right now, I'm about two minutes away from the churchyard in Low Scaraby. I just hope Spadework will talk to me."

Becky clicked the recorder off. As she turned the bend, the top of St Bosco's church came into view in the distance.

***

Jack spoke to himself with only Fletcher, the black rabbit, to hear. "That's everything. An owl's feather at each cardinal point, a circle of salt at the centre, my runes laid out counter witch-wise around a candle." He nodded and tried to think back to the last time he had needed to contact someone using the spirit dial method. It was so outdated. He took out his notes. "Here goes." He took a breath.

"Isse-ven turundig viri selib spiritus ortas rubeum pa-larum unwitch!" He waited a moment and thought he heard a crackle in the air. "I say again: Isse-ven turundig viri selib spiritus ortas rubeum pa-larum unwitch!"

This time the air did crackle, Jack felt his moustache quiver and everything in the Nissen hut rattled. The crackle turned to a more distinct hiss of white noise, like a television needing to be tuned. Gradually the noise dissipated as a bright bluish glow began to emanate from the centre of Jack's circle of sorcery. A figure appeared, a little distorted but a figure nonetheless, and he wore a fedora.

"What on earth?" said the man with the fedora.

"Whitaker! Is that you? Can you see me? Do you hear me?" Despite the fuzziness of the image Jack recognised his Unwitcher colleague.

"Jack Baxter? Of course! The dishonoured and disgraced Unwitcher drags my aura into a spirit call! You will not win, you realise? You have only assured your own annihilation!"

Jack realised his heart was pumping harder than the time he fought a vampiric rat in the tunnels beneath Lytham St Annes. "Whitaker, please you must listen to me – I am not the enemy. I have not taken Zelementra."

Whitaker puffed himself up. "You are a darkness within the world of Unwitching and we are the light that shall vanquish you!"

Jack shook his head. "You must listen. You have been deceived – we all have. It is Gravestone Sam, he has returned and made you believe I have taken Zelementra. It is Gravestone Sam!"

Whitaker shook his head and his glowing image lost focus for a moment. "Gravestone Sam was banished to the Void by Zelementra herself. You are playing games, just as you have always played games."

Jack could see that his runes were floating now above the concrete floor, their circle beginning to break. His connection wouldn't last long. "Listen to me then, you pompous bunch-backed toad! I want you to try and save Zelementra and I want you to try and stop me. None of you useless excuses for Unwitchers can manage it, even though I'm going to make it easy for you."

Whitaker began to bluster but Jack shouted over his noise.

"I'm in the East Midlands, not Galdoun Castle. I'm in Mercia Quadrant Five, between the villages of Hexhorn and Low Scaraby. I want this showdown so you'd better get yourselves here as soon as you can."

"By my hat!" said Whitaker, pulling the fedora from his head in anger. "You have some nerve, Jack Baxter!"

"Mercia Quadrant Five," Jack told him again and then kicked the runes and candle causing Whitaker's image to disappear and everything to become silent.

"Idiots," Jack muttered to himself in the darkness.

***

"Oh hey magpie! Speak with me this morning. Ho hey magpie, wiser than an owl."

Becky stopped, feeling foolish. She wasn't sure if she had remembered the song quite right or if it would even work this time and without Jack. She took a breath and resumed.

"Ho hey magpie! Speak with me this morning. Ho hey magpie, more handsome than a robin.

Ho hey magpie! It is the morning hour. Ho hey. Magpie?"

Becky looked about her. The graveyard did not feel scary, only solitary and it was that which made her feel afraid – there was only her and the gravestones and an ever-increasing sense that time was running out to save Zelementra, and possibly this reality as well.

From above her there came a rustling of tree branches and then a hoarse cry of a magpie. Spadework was suddenly settling on to a gravestone just in front of Becky and folding his wings.

"Argh. It's you again," he said. "The Unwitcher's non-apprentice."

"It's Becky," she told the bird. "My name is Becky."

"Becky," the bird nodded. "Non-apprentice Unwitcher's servant."

She stepped toward him, unable to go on pretending she wasn't desperate. "Oh, Spadework. I need your help. Please help me."

He cocked his head. "Don't you have any normal clothes?"

"Sorry?"

"Earlier it was pyjamas and now you're dressed like a farmer."

"It's been a terrible morning," she said, realising the truth of it. "That's why I'm here again."

"You mean because of Gravestone Sam."

"Yes. He's kidnapped Zelementra, but he's also luring all the Unwitcher's into a trap. He's going to destroy everything and turn this realm into…into something monstrous."

"Argh. He's a jumped-up little hellion."

"Spadework, will you help me?"

"And why isn't the Unwitcher here himself?"

Becky moved closer to the bird. "Jack doesn't know I've come to you. When I left, he was trying to make contact with another Unwitcher, trying to explain what is going on."

"Argh. They won't believe him."

"So will you help me or not." Her frustration was beginning to turn to anger.

"There are rules that must be followed…"

"What does it matter about bloody rules! If Gravestone Sam gets his way, your stupid

Unwitcher rules won't matter. Nothing will matter because everything will be…"

"Destroyed," Spadework interrupted.

Becky looked at the bird and the bird looked at Becky. "Doesn't that mean anything to you?" she asked.

"Argh. If you let me finish, I was going to say that rules must be followed but this is an exceptional situation. You may not be an Unwitcher but you have the pig-headedness of one! Yes, I will help you."

Becky felt some of the tension in her body leave. "Thank you, Spadework. Thank you."

"And if we aren't destroyed," the bird added, "I will expect you to bring me a very big shiny. A very shiny shiny."

"Anything you want."

"Excellent!" Spadework hopped and flapped and came to rest on the top of Becky's head.

"We need to find out exactly where Sam is keeping Zelementra," Becky told him, feeling awkward but reassured. "All I know is it is somewhere inside The Barley Triangle."

"That would make sense. The triangle is a place of bad energies. We magpies avoid it."

Becky thought. "Zelementra made some sort of psychic connection with Jack. She was very weak, but she said she was being held in an old barn."

"Argh. The other day I spoke with my friend, Meridian the Owl. She told me she had noticed hoof prints of a Kastrian Demon near to an old gamekeeper's hut. It is in the middle of the triangle. It has been empty for many a year."

Becky no longer thought it strange that an owl might talk, not even that it had talked with a magpie. "Do you know this place?"

"Yes. It is very isolated and on the far, far edge of Scaraby Woods. Meridian is very old, and her sight is poor, so I did not pay it much mind. Now though, it sounds as if she was right about the hoof marks."

Becky began to feel a small sense of hope. She went and sat on a nearby bench and Spadework moved to rest upon her lap. "Well," she said. "The hut sounds like a good place to start."

"You must be careful."

"How do I get there?"

Spadework cocked his head. "It would be much easier if you could fly."

"I don't have wings, but I do have a Polo with a dodgy handbrake and a half tank of petrol. Can you guide me?"

"Argh. I'm not getting in a car."

"But I'll get lost without your help."

Spadework took off for a gravestone and lighted upon the cracked vertical of a cross. "I am a magpie of the sky and the fields," he told her, folding his wings again.

"And now my passenger seat," Becky declared. "We don't have much time."

"Argh! The indignity. I had better get a very impressive shiny!"

"You will. I promise."

***

Jack was surprised at himself. As he trudged along a narrow trackway, not far from Scaraby Woods, he contemplated the situation and found himself wishing that Becky was with him. She had proved herself to be a spirited and capable partner and he had begun to value her presence – but he could not have waited any longer for her. Gravestone Sam had to be destroyed.

He stopped and checked the old map he had brought with him. There was an old gamekeeper's hut marked on it – Jack decided, given everything they knew, this was probably the best place to start. His Unwitcher instinct told him it had to be where Zelementra was. Just a few more minutes down the track, then into a copse of trees and he would be there. He put the map back in his coat pocket and noticed how dark the sky had gotten. On he went, trying to ignore the knot of fear that had grown in his stomach.

"Look," cried a gaggle of tiny voices. "It's an Unwitcher!"

Jack looked down. "Black Magic Mushrooms," he sighed, seeing the self-important patch of purple on the ground ahead of him.

"That's right!" the voices responded. "You want to lick us don't you!"

"No. Not especially."

"Come on, you old badger! Give us a lick and take the trip of a lifetime."

Jack shook his head. "How many patches of you things are there?"

"Haha!" they chorused. "Our mycelium stretches through the earth like a brightly coloured nightmare you will never wake up from. Come on – taste our caps!"

"At least I must be on the right track," Jack said it to himself more than to the mushrooms.

"You certainly are, you poor fool," they told him. "Gravestone Sam is expecting you."

He crouched down. "You think that surprises me?"

The mushrooms laughed. "We think it scares you."

"Well, that shows how limited your collective brain is."

"We are superior! When Gravestone Sam finishes with you, he'll turn you into mulch and feed your remains to us."

Jack had an idea. He grabbed hold of a handful of the mushrooms and stuffed them into his handkerchief and then into his pocket. The remaining mushrooms shouted that they were going to get him. Jack ignored them and walked on. "I don't have time for this."

Five minutes later he was crouched behind a fallen log covered in ferns. Ahead of him was the hut. He waited, expecting to see Kastrian demons on patrol, but there was no sign of any. There was, in fact, no sign of any kind of creature, otherworldly or native. Not even a crow. Something wasn't right. Jack's Astral Hexatic Compass was glowing green with a reading of zero. He'd never known that to happen before. Absolute zero. It didn't matter. Trap or not, he knew he could wait no longer. Whatever happened he was going inside. Jack stood from behind the fronds of fern and crept toward the ramshackle door of the hut.

"Hello?" he whispered, stepping inside. "Is anyone in here?"

As his eyes began adjusting to the gloom he heard a groaning sound, then he saw a figure slumped in the corner. It was her!

"Zelementra! Thank Hermes you are still alive. Is your mind intact or am I too late?" He went to her.

She managed to lift her head. "Grandmother!" She smiled at him. "I'm so glad to see you!"

"Sorry?"

"Those butterflies on your dress are so wonderful." Zelementra took his hand.

"We need to get out of here," he told her. "Before Sam and who knows what else appear."

Zelementra continued to smile at him.

"At least your mind is still processing," he nodded, relieved.

"Be honest," she told him with a frown. "Did you make that dress yourself?"

"Well, sort of processing." He put his arm around her and was about to try and get her to her feet.

There was a creaking noise and Gravestone Sam was standing in the doorway. "At last," he said. "Jack Baxter, the great Unwitcher, has arrived."

Jack turned to see the demon, his toupee still ridiculous, the smug look upon his face still irksome. "Gravestonne Sam," he replied. "You little toad."

Sam sighed and stepped further into the hut. "Your jibes continue to show a lack of imagination, matched only by your wardrobe. I believe you were wearing that same tatty old coat the last time we met."

"You mean when Zelementra and I banished you into the Void."

"And yet, here I am standing before you." He made a show of being stood before him.

"If it's hurting your neck looking up at me, I can crouch."

Gravestone Sam made a sudden leap on to a roof beam above Jack's head. His eyes glowed with an orange fire, momentarily. "You really don't understand, do you?" he said with a snarl. "If you fully understood the situation, you wouldn't be making such jokes at my expense."

Jack thought about making a quip along the lines that Sam had such a *short* temper but didn't. Instead, the smile fell from his face. Sam was right after all. This was probably the worst situation Jack had found himself in for a very long time.

"No," said Sam, carrying on. "If you did understand you would have soiled yourself by now. Although, it looks as if you already have." He looked down on the stain at the front of Jack's trousers.

"Actually, that's smeared Black Magic Mushrooms. I crushed a few on way here."

Sam laughed and stomped a foot on the wooden beam, shaking loose some of its dust. "Is that supposed to impress me?"

"If it weakens the strength of the juice you've clearly fed to Zelementra, even just a little bit, then that's something. I'll take any positive I can get."

"Well one small patch means nothing. I've been cultivating mushrooms for weeks. The poor old girl won't be coming back to earth for quite some time."

Jack was about to call him a bastard when Zelementra joined the conversation.

"Now, will you two just pack it in or I'll send you to your rooms. My programme is about to start so just make friends or you can go to bloody bed!"

"He started it!" Sam declared.

"Look what you've done to her." Jack knelt by her side again.

"Isn't it brilliant? You have no idea how long I've been planning this - preparing my return."

Jack shook his head. "Your return ends here."

Sam dropped down to the floor. His hair did not move. "I wonder when you're going to work any of this out. You won't at all." He decided with a nod. "I'm just going to have to tell you. That's fine. More fun anyway."

Jack looked into his eyes, still with that frightful orange glow burning within them. "Look, I'm taking Zelementra and we're both getting out of here."

"Do you hear that?" Sam raised a finger. "That's the noise of an assortment of demons surrounding this hut. Neither of you are going anywhere.

Jack could hear it. A vicious snorting of something short tempered and bestial. He knew Sam wasn't bluffing.

"Which of you two gentleman is going to take my ticket" Zelementra enquired. "I mustn't miss this train."

"Her mind won't last much longer." Jack felt a desperation well up inside him.

"A shame isn't it."

Jack held her cheek in his palm and forced her to look into his eyes. "Your name is Zelementra. You are the head of the Guild of Unwitcher's. You run the Guild. Your name is Zelementra!

Her expression glazed with no understanding.

"She trapped me in the void," Sam said bitterly. "And you helped her."

"You were a menace. We couldn't leave you roaming in the world.

"Both of you put me in that place."

"You had to be gotten rid of."

"Well, my time in the Void was not wasted. I grew stronger in there. I had to, alone in the nothingness with only other damaged entities for company. It truly was terrible and for someone like me, someone who had been down there," he pointed to the floor, "with the board of diabolic directors, looking on at this terrible shitshow of a reality, whilst sat next to the king of all mischief. I went from that to nothing. The Void certainly showed me what absolute darkness can be."

"I'm not going to allow you to have your silly revenge. Understand?" Jack tried to sound confident.

Gravestone Sam became more annoyed. "It is you who does not understand. I have orchestrated everything to bring you here."

Jack began to think he could jump the little sprite, make a surprise move and stuff his stupid wig down his throat. He stayed still though and kept hold of Zelementra's hand. He knew that, ultimately, it would be futile to attack Sam now. The green and unpleasant demon was far stronger than he looked and had powers which had only gotten stronger since his escape from the Void.

"You remember the great Mystagogue Ball?" Sam asked.

"Of course."

The sprite sniggered. "I doubt you can remember very much at all. Do you have a recollection of insulting all your other Unwitchers or the Magpie King? You annoyed so many that night."

"It was you, wasn't it!"

"Yes. I saw to it that your drink was spiked. I must say, even I was surprised at how irritating and impertinent you became. It couldn't have worked out better."

Jack stepped toward the sprite, unable any longer to restrain the temptation to kick his face. But, with a simple wave of his squamous green hand, Sam sent Jack tumbling to the floor with a powerful blast of energy.

"After the scene you caused at the ball," Sam went on, "Zelementra would have to make an example of you and send you off somewhere. I know how she thinks. Once I knew the exact quadrant she was sending you to, that's when my plan really swung into action."

Jack's whole body felt as if he had been tossed against an electric fence. He strained to lift his head. "How could I have been so blind?"

"Arrogance. Stupidity. Take your pick. And don't think your little companion, Becky, is going to come to your rescue either."

"What?"

"Yes, I know all about her too. Her car has been located in Low Scaraby and I have dispatched some demons to take care of her."

"But that's not possible!" Jack pulled himself up and dragged himself closer to Zelementra.

Sam smiled at the scene. "I knew explaining everything would be most satisfying."

Jack grasped Zelementra's hand. It seemed to bring her mind back for just a moment. "Oh, Jack," she said with genuine fear in her voice. "I think Gravestone Sam might have escaped from the Void. He wants to destroy us, Jack. He's going to wipe us all out!"

Part Six:

It Gets Dark. It Gets Lonely

The air was cold around her ears. Becky gripped the crate tighter and tried to enjoy the view. "How high are we?" she shouted to Spadework.

"The fall would kill you," he told her. "Unless you fell through those trees down there – that wouldn't kill you, but it would hurt a lot."

"Right." Becky had hoped for a more straightforward answer and considered whether she should just keep her eyes closed. "I am grateful to you and...did you say they were your nephews?" She glanced back at the two birds flying behind her, their beaks holding two thin ropes tied to the crate.

Spadework was at the front. He held a third rope from his feet. "Argh. They are the juveniles of my brother Scattergun," he told her. "They are young and strong. Just stay still and don't move about."

"Don't worry, I'm not going to move one bit." The crate caught the wind and swung to the left and the two younger magpies let out a disgruntled cry. "Have you done this before?" Becky asked Spadework, still unsure how he had talked her into being transported through the air in a crate they had retrieved from a nearby farmyard.

"I once transported a brood of badger cubs using a basket and rope method, and once the mummified remains of a cat, but never a human. You are the heaviest."

"Oh," was all Becky could manage.

"We are nearly at the gamekeeper's hut. Do you see it? A little further ahead. I told you this is the quickest way to get to it."

She peeked over the basket. "Yes. Oh my god! What are they?"

"Argh. It looks as if there is an assortment of demons surrounding the hut."

"It has to be the right place then."

"Gravestone Sam must be inside with Zelementra," Spadework agreed.

"We've got to scare those things off."

"Leave that to us. We will fly at the beasts and the stupid creatures will chase after us."

Becky looked down and thought of Jack and hoped that he might suddenly appear from out of the trees and send all the creatures back to whichever dimension they came from, but there was no sign of him.

The magpies began to arc away from the hut. "Do you see the old stone trough in the corner of that field?" Spadework asked.

"Yes, I see it."

"We will land you next to it. Then, if you run along the field's edge it will bring you to the hut."

"Right." Becky took a deep breath and felt the cold air enter her lungs and chill the heat in her blood. Her heart jumped.

"Don't delay," Spadework told her. "Get Zelementra and get away as soon as you can. We can only distract the demons for so long."

"Spadework, I don't know if I'm ready for this. I should have paid more attention to the things Jack told me about these spirits and demons and the occult." She felt her body beginning to tremble.

"Argh! Don't be such a bore. None of that matters. You can do this. You must do this."

"Yes."

"Fail and we're all doomed anyway."

"I know."

The birds slid down through the sky and the earth came closer, the hedgerows regained their detailed arterial form, and the air took on the scent of mud and vegetation. The crate touched the ground with a bump.

"I have one last piece of advice," Spadework said, dropping the rope and fluttering to rest on the side of the crate. "Sam was a sprite of Satan and one thing that sprites of Satan cannot stand are high pitched noises. If things go bad, just scream and shriek as loudly as you can. It won't destroy him, but it might be enough to disorientate him so that you can fly away."

Becky thought for a moment. "So, you're saying if things go badly, I should start screaming?"

"Yes."

"I think I can remember that." Becky climbed from the crate.

"Argh. Good luck."

***

Jack had begun to feel weak. Gravestone Sam was still pontificating about his revenge and talking and talking of his immense cunning and saying things about bringing everything to a close and the Unwitchers demise, and how he had been pulling the strings for so long.

Jack fell to his knees as everything in the hut started to become a little fuzzier. He looked over to Zelementra. Once again, she didn't seem to know where she was. She couldn't last much longer.

"Everything the Unwitcher stands for and the membrane between worlds, which you all so valiantly guard," Sam said, with a small green finger pointing in the air, "is about to be torn down and set light to."

Jack looked at the finger, pointing upwards, followed its direction and saw that above the rafters was an altar of sorts, suspended like a chandelier. It was circular and made of stone – a mill stone! Upon it, in what appeared to be dried blood, was drawn a symbol. Even as his mind grew more clouded, Jack knew exactly what it was. A sigil. The sigil of Baphomet, a mark of ancient origin, of mysticism and balance and a powerful symbol used in the ritual to cast one into the Void. Jack understood then. The hut was a cage, a cauldron into which the ingredients for a magical working had been prepared. The sigil had been enervating Zelementra, just as it had begun to enfeeble him. From outside a wind had begun to swirl.

"An eye for an eye, a claw for a claw!" Sam laughed. "You shall both be trapped in the Void for time without end. Enjoy your stay in the darkness of the damned and the nothingness. I suppose living here has prepared you for it." He laughed again as a crackling noise filled the hut. The mill stone above them started to tremor and its dry blood sigil began to glow beetroot red.

Jack looked to Zelementra. Her eyes had closed. He tried to stand but his legs would not move.

The door to the hut flung open. In the boiler suit that Jack had given her, stood Becky. She looked stunned. "Right!" she declared. "Er, everyone stay where you are." She observed the strange scene in front of her.

Sam turned around. "Who are you? The farmer?"

She looked down to where the voice had come from and saw the thing that must have been Gravestone Sam, surprised by his wig and green skin and small stature. "I've already dealt with those demons out there and now it's your turn!" she told him.

"You're just brimming with confidence aren't you! What is your name farmhand?"

"My name is Becky and I'm here for my friends."

"They certainly must be your friends – you are all very tiresome. Well, you can join them. It's all the same to me." Sam clicked his fingers and Becky was lifted from the floor and thrown across the hut to where Jack and Zelementra floundered.

"Ianis farigh gwagle!" Sam cried and from the sigil stone above erupted a violet beam that filled the entire space. Everything began to shudder. Sam adjusted his hairpiece and continued to shout his incantation.

Becky pulled herself closer to Jack and clutched at his duffle coat.

"You should not have come," he told her.

"I went to get help," she explained. "I've seen Spadework. He brought me here." The purple light was everywhere, it was as if they had suddenly found themselves in some awful, throbbing nightclub where the music was a dark, jarring drone. "What's happening, Jack? My whole body feels weird, like everything is fizzing."

Jack breathed heavily. "Sam is using his necromantic powers to send us to the Void, the place between worlds. He's draining us, pulling us into the nothing."

"I wanted to rescue Zelementra," she told him. "I wanted to help."

Jack reached into his pocket. All his bones and tendons were beginning to ache. "If I can get to Sam, I think I can stop him. In my pocket I have the remains of some Black Magic mushrooms. I have altered them with a spell. If Sam ingests it, the modified compound should stun him for a moment, like an electrode through his brain. It should be enough to halt the incantation."

"I can distract him," Becky said. "Something which Spadework told me. Did you know Sam cannot stand high pitched noises? Jack?"

The Unwitcher did not answer. He had started to fade. In the purple light, his skin had turned pale and translucent in patches. His face was disappearing.

Becky knew she had to act. She pulled herself to her feet and stepped toward the demon. Sam had finished his incantation and was holding on to his hair as the hut rattled ever more furiously.

"Well, aren't you a stubborn little stain," he said, seeing Becky standing before him. "I'll soon have you out. Give my regards to the nothingness."

Becky thrust her arms out at her side and began to sing as loudly as she could. "Out on the wily, windy moors we'd roll and fall in green! Ooh-ahh, ooh-ahh, a -woo! Do do do do do do do dooo!"

Sam staggered back, his hair falling off. "Stop it! The noise. The terrible noise!"

Becky continued. "Ooh-ah, ooh-ah, a-woo! Ooh it gets dark, it gets lonely, on the other side from you."

"Please stop!"

The purple light flickered, and Sam stumbled sideways. Jack made it to his feet and was at him in an instant with a ball of black sludge in his hand. He grabbed the demon by his neck. "Here, take a taste of your own mushroom medicine with a twist of Unwitcher!" Jack shoved the sludge into the unwilling mouth of Gravestone Sam, forcing it in and forcing his jaw closed. Demon and Unwitcher fell down together, and Jack let his weight fall on top of the creature. The purple light emanating from the sigil stone above was like a strobe light now and everything moved in slow motion.

"Everything is shimmering," Sam cried when Jack let go of his jaw. "Everything is fruity!"

"It's working!" Jack called out. "Get Zelementra."

Becky was already at her side, scooping her up into her arms.

Jack looked into the eyes of Gavestone Sam. Their orange glow had gone and had been replaced by only black.

"I'm waiting for the milkman and mother will be ever so disappointed if my shoes aren't clean," the demon told the Unwitcher. "Curse you," he hissed. Gravestone Sam clutched at Jack's wrists. "Curse all the Unwitchers."

The hut began to shudder uncontrollably. Chunks of plaster and roof tiles fell to the floor. The strobing purple light had ceased, its wavelength had changed. Everything now glowed red.

"Jack!" Becky screamed, "the stone is coming down!"

Above them, the huge millstone, with the sigil of Baphomet in blood, had broken free of the ropes which suspended it. For a moment it appeared to hover in the air but just as the roof of the hut began to collapse and the walls began to tumble, so too did the mill stone fall.

Jack turned to Becky who had thrown Zelementra over her shoulder. "Get out!" he told her. As the millstone crashed it pulled everything else down with it, including the floor. It was as if the earth coughed and spluttered and then swallowed a great brown blob of phlegm.

***

"Argh! That is a very big mess you have created," Spadework said. He was sitting on

Jack's shoulder, looking at the space where the gamekeeper's hut had stood for more years than anyone could remember. Dust and sulphuric smoke still drifted up from the freshly ploughed wound. "It's like a mass grave. Look, there's the top of a tree sticking out of it. That old oak must have been thirty feet tall."

There were three people staring at the unsettled earth. It was as if they were mourners at the side of a recently filled grave. A recently filled grave that was very large and had almost swallowed them. Not only had the hut been pulled down into the earth but a good deal of the trees around it also.

"Argh. It is a grave for Gravestone Sam all right."

"Let us hope so," Zelementra said quietly. She rested herself on the ground and had Jack's coat around her shoulders. She felt weak, as if having woken from a fever, but her mind had returned, and her thoughts were her own once more. "We cannot allow ourselves to underestimate that heinous sprite."

"I saw the stone fall down onto his weakened body." Jack said. "He was already partway into the Void that he had conjured with his own magic. Gravestone Sam is gone. He has to be."

No one said anything for a moment.

"It's a good job that Becky and I saved everybody, isn't it." Spadework decided.

Jack tried to grab the bird, but he fluttered off to a nearby gatepost.

"Spadework is correct," Zelementra smiled. "We must all be grateful to him and Becky,"

"And just like that the Unwitcher's contribution is ignored. That's so typical! If only I had sung a Kate Bush song!"

"Don't be grumpy, Jack, and help me up." Zelementra reached out to her Unwitcher and he took her hand and gently helped her to her feet.

"But are you certain," Becky asked, still staring at the barrow they had created. "What if Gravestone Sam isn't in the Void? What if he's in there?" She pointed toward the ruffled earth. "Or what if he just got away? I mean, none of us really saw what happened. We were just trying to get out before everything got swallowed up."

"I can no longer sense him," Zelementra said, closing her eyes. "That is a good sign."

"Yes," said Spadework, "the air feels clearer."

"What about all the Kastrian demons and whatever else?" Becky asked, still not convinced.

"They will have vanished along with their master, or were destroyed when the portal closed," Jack told her. "If there are any left, without Sam, they won't last long."

"You have all done very well, under the circumstances," Zelementra told them.

"Please tell that to all of the other Unwitchers," Jack said, sounding grumpy once again. "They have demonstrated just how bloody useless they are."

Zelementra leaned on Becky's shoulder for support. "That's enough, Jack," she reprimanded. "Once I return to our Doncaster offices, I shall make it quite clear to the others what has happened here and what lessons we can all learn from it."

"But you aren't leaving yet, are you?" Becky asked.

Zelementra took her hand. "No, I shall rest for a day or two here until my strength returns and the mushroom juice fully leaves my system."

"Then, I too shall soon be leaving this quadrant." Jack turned away from the mound with a sigh. He no longer wanted to look at it.

"No Jack, not straight away." Zelementra said with a slight smile.

"But surely my work here is done?" Jack protested to his boss. "I saved you and all the other Unwitchers and this whole reality for that matter!" He gestured at the trees and the fields that were all about them. "I think I've earned a little holiday."

"You are now more important than ever," Zelementra said soothingly. "We can't expect Spadework to patrol this area all by himself."

Spadework flew to Zelementra and landed on her shoulder. "I could though," he told her. "This is my domain, and I can keep a very close eye on everything for you."

"I know you could. You are a valiant magpie indeed. But I think Mercia Quadrant Five needs a designated Unwitcher now. In this place the veil has been abused and weakened. More than ever, we must be vigilant and more than ever there should be an Unwitcher and perhaps, an apprentice." She turned and smiled at Becky.

"What!" Becky and Jack both spluttered.

"Becky has shown herself to be more than capable," Zelementra went on. "She is just the sort of person we need to invigorate the Guild. And an apprentice would need a master to guide her."

"Argh! I think it's a very good idea," Spadework said, taking to the air.

Becky beamed and hugged Zelementra. "I'm so grateful. I don't know what to say. I don't know if I can accept it. Could it work?"

"You must take your time and think things over. There is no need to decide right away, but you and Jack clearly work well together. I believe in your capabilities Becky. You could be a great Unwitcher with the right guidance."

"Hang on a minute," Jack demanded. "Don't I get any say in this? What if I don't want to stay here? What if I don't want an apprentice?"

"Come on now, Jack," Zelementra smiled more broadly. "Don't be so sour. I think it would be wonderful."

He took his coat from her shoulders and put it back on. "This is ridiculous," he said walking off toward the woods, stuffing his hands in his pockets.

Becky and Zelementra walked after him. "Don't worry, Jack," Becky shouted. "You know I pick things up quickly and I'll be gentle with you. I promise!"

Jack kept walking with Spadework fluttering above him.

"Argh. I think it's a very good idea," the magpie kept saying. "A very good idea indeed!"

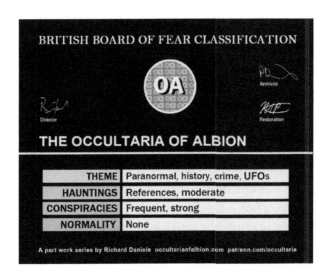

BRITISH BOARD OF FEAR CLASSIFICATION

OA

Archivist

Director

Restoration

THE OCCULTARIA OF ALBION

THEME	Paranormal, history, crime, UFOs
HAUNTINGS	References, moderate
CONSPIRACIES	Frequent, strong
NORMALITY	None

A part work series by Richard Daniels occultariaofalbion.com patreon.com/occultaria

If you have enjoyed this book and would like to know more about Unwitching and the world of the Occultaria of Albion, why not join the fan club and become an OAKnight! You will receive lots of exclusive material and a monthly newsletter.

Just go to:

www.patreon.com/occultaria

Richard Daniels is a writer and the archivist for all the surviving files and documents of the Occultaria of Albion. He was given the archive by one of the original writers and creators of the part work series, Nigel Fenwick.

From his home in the Lincolnshire Wolds, Richard continues to investigate, write and speak about the paranormal, supernatural and folkloric phenomena which the Occultaria of Albion first explored more than forty years ago.

He lives with and is aided by the artist, Melody Phelan-Clark.

Acknowledgements

I would like to thank the residents of Hexhorn and Low Scaraby for their hospitality and patience.

I am full of joy, gratitude and love to Melody for being a part of everything. Thank you

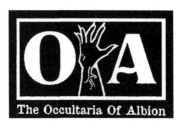

The Occultaria Of Albion

Follow:

 @oa.richarddaniels

 @occultaria

occultariaofalbion.com

Printed in Great Britain
by Amazon

36980697R00078